1984

Michael A. ███████tti
117 Seeser Street
Joliet, Illinois 60435█

THE INDIAN SIGN

A  BOOK

Books by John Gunther

Public Affairs

Inside Europe
(First published 1936, repeatedly revised and republished)
Inside Asia
(First published 1939, revised 1942)
Inside Latin America
Inside U.S.A.
(First published 1947, revised 1951)
Inside Africa
Inside Russia Today
Inside Europe Today
(First published 1961, revised and republished 1962)
Inside South America

Biography

Death Be Not Proud
Roosevelt in Retrospect
The Riddle of MacArthur
Eisenhower: The Man and the Symbol
Taken at the Flood: The Story of Albert D. Lasker
Procession

Autobiography

A Fragment of Autobiography: The Fun of Writing the *Inside* Books

Novels

The Red Pavilion
Peter Lancelot
The Golden Fleece
The Bright Nemesis
The Troubled Midnight
The Lost City
The Indian Sign

Reporting

The High Cost of Hitler
D Day
Behind the Curtain

Miscellaneous

Days to Remember
(With Bernard Quint)
Chicago Revisited

Juveniles

Alexander the Great
Julius Caesar
The Golden Fleece
Meet North Africa
(With Sam and Beryl Epstein)
Meet South Africa
(With Sam and Beryl Epstein)
Meet the Congo and Its Neighbors
Meet Soviet Russia
(Two volumes)

Travel

Twelve Cities

THE
INDIAN SIGN

A NOVEL BY

JOHN GUNTHER

1817

HARPER & ROW, PUBLISHERS

NEW YORK, EVANSTON

AND LONDON

FIRST EDITION

LIBRARY OF CONGRESS CATALOG CARD NUMBER: 71–108945

Dedicated to A. K. W. and the memory of Mac

THE INDIAN SIGN

A  BOOK

1

He had his Pulitzer—mine was still to come. Not that competition on this level mattered in the least; we were as close as brothers, more so than most brothers. Besides, he was a man of the typewriter, first and last, whereas I had gone into this new thing, radio. He pretended to despise radio, but he was impressed by the amount of money I made—although he was probably the highest-paid American newspaper correspondent on the continent at that time.

"Radio stinks," said Mac. "Your rating depends on who's your competition, not on your own value or merit. As a matter of fact, it depends on who precedes you too, because people are too lazy to turn off sets. Besides, the listener can't reread your copy, he can't check back, he can't refer to a text or keep it on the record."

I said nothing.

"Am I right?" he snapped amiably, "or am I right?"

"Right."

"Well, smile."

This was in September, 1939, and World War II had just begun. We stood side by side on the tender, grinding its way toward the S.S. *Rotterdam* anchored off Southampton. This was a Dutch ship, of neutral registry, and would presumably be safe for the voyage unless some U-boat commander lost his head. The *Rotterdam* looked like a huge postcard out there in the water. No other craft was near. A steady straight rain drove nails into the water.

I braced myself on a large wooden case which held some pictures I had bought at the Leicester Galleries in London a day or two before. There hadn't been time or opportunity to ship them, and Mac and I had to hire a light truck to carry them to Southampton. We rode with the truck. That cluster of paintings, bought on the edge of the moment and without expert advice, proved to be the best investment I ever made, or my name is not Nelson A. Nelson. I don't think that the Braque cost more than a hundred pounds, and the last time I had it appraised for the insurance it was valued at $28,500.

My interest in this was not, however, fiduciary in the least; Elspeth always says that I have no sense of money. Money is what's fun to spend.

I stepped out to the greasy foredeck of the tender, and Mac supported my elbow with his strong, sinewy, and fraternal grip. Casually he tapped my left ankle with the blackthorn he always carried (in those old days), and the crack of wood on wood was resounding, almost cheerful. Mac had cost me that foot in an automobile accident in the Tyrol a couple of years before. He always drove too fast. Having cost me my foot gave him a considerable sense of guilt, which he dissembled. I felt guilty about his having the sense of guilt.

At this particular time I was somewhat worried about Mac, because he was drinking far too much. The tremor in his fingers, which the doctors said was irreversible, seemed to be more pronounced than ever. A disconcerting small episode had just occurred. I was having dinner in London with Gilmore Scott of the UP and his wife, and, quite late, at about two in the morning, we decided on impulse to root Mac out of bed. Karen was in Paris, and he was staying at the Connaught alone.

He woke up after we banged on the door a longish time, and we sat around chatting for an hour. He was alert, deft, gay. With pride and pleasure he showed Enid Scott some antique jewels and *objets d'art* he had just bought at Cameo Corner for his mother, fondling them affectionately. Then he went into a long, careful, discerning analysis of the military situation in Poland; he was one of the few correspondents with enough savvy to predict that the Poles would scarcely be able to hold out a week against the invading Nazis. Such arrant pessimism disturbed us all.

3

We made an engagement for lunch the next day, but he didn't show. After half an hour I telephoned him. Not only had he completely forgotten about the luncheon date, but he had no memory at all of our visit during the night. Every detail was blotted out. It was as if we had never been there. His behavior had been absolutely rational while we were there, but now he remembered nothing. I was startled and upset. It seemed inconceivable that he could remember nothing at all.

As we approached the *Rotterdam,* I saw her first, standing against the rail on an upper deck—a tallish girl with chestnut hair, a lovely forehead, dark eyes, and a luminous glossy quality that seemed to give a note of willingness to the skin. The explanation of all this is simple. The MacIntyres lived in Paris, and, because Mac thought that the Germans would attack and take Paris practically at once, he decided that his family had better go home for a while. So Karen and their two children, Prince and Devlin, around five and three, contrived to get passage on the *Rotterdam,* and had joined the ship that morning at Le Havre. Mac had moved to London, because this would be the best springboard for the Allied invasion of the continent which, we all thought, would come at any moment. Now Mac was meeting Karen and the children for a brief glimpse to see them off, and would return to London that night. London was blanketed with security regulations, and he had had to go all the way to Churchill (who had just come back to government as First Lord) himself to obtain permission to board the *Rotterdam*, even briefly, as it paused in British waters before crossing the Atlantic. On account of the war, flying was impossible at just that moment.

"Nelson!" exclaimed Karen, with her level warm wide smile. "How nice of you to help see me off."

"I'm not seeing you off. I'm a fellow passenger."

"How come?" Even with words as banal, as brief as these, her voice had a stirring quality, something both reserved and beckoning.

"Elspeth's sick. I hate to miss the beginning of the war, but duty calls. She needs me, not that she'd admit it, and I really have to see her."

I had had a cablegram the day before from a doctor somewhere in Maine, up in the woods, to the effect that Elspeth had just had an emergency operation for a burst appendix, and was dangerously ill. The cablegram was addressed to my London bank. I found out later that Elspeth had refused, when she was conscious, to give the doctor my address—out of perversity or perhaps because she did not want to disturb me or interrupt my work—and he had located me only by rummaging through her things and finding an old British checkbook. The last direct word I had had from her was a cable, typical of all her humanitarianism, "CRY PEACE," some days before.

"Well," said Karen, with that low mellow voice, "I'm sorry, and I hope she'll be all right."

Of course Karen was sorry, but she and Elspeth

5

were not particularly close, although they got along well enough when they met. Karen was not a girl to have friendships with other women. Elspeth admired Karen, but was jealous of her as well. Among other things she resented the MacIntyres' extravagance. Once they drove all the way up to a place we had in Connecticut (which we sold later) in a taxi they had picked up on Times Square. Expenditure on such a scale affronted Elspeth, a puritan to the bone. Then, too, Karen was too earthy for Elspeth, who was an undine, a water sprite. Although I was bound to Elspeth by a hugely complicated web of comradeship, affection, guilt, group associations, respect, admiration, love—yes, even love—I was much closer to Mac and Karen. For years we had been a threesome. We went everywhere together. I suppose I was in love with them both, and they were both very fond of me.

Elspeth, my wife, stood in a category all her own. She lived an altogether different kind of life. It did not amuse her to sit up in bars all night, gossip with the brethren, and take mad junkets to Zagreb, Lwów, or Ankara. It did not impress her in the least that Mac had written two quite good books—novels. She didn't drink. She was totally serious—an intellectual. I suppose her dominant qualities were reserve, based on sensitiveness, and a compelling addiction to paradox. She lacked the capacity for easy choice, which I have always thought was a particular stigma of the

6

neurotic. Mac said once, "She's a witch, but you're still in love with her, and she *loves* you."

I liked my cabin on the *Rotterdam,* and I unpacked a few things slowly. My leg hurt as I clambered to the forward bar to join Mac and Karen there.

2

The three of us, comfortable with the satisfactions of our relationship, secure, fond, had double stingers in the bar, whereupon, after twenty minutes, Mac rose abruptly. "We have some money things to talk about," he explained, leading Karen away. She looked lissome. I think "lissome" is one of the worst words in the English language, but that was what she was, with her delicate high well-separated breasts over a slim waist. Almost never did she wear a brassiere. They came back from Karen's cabin an hour later. As a rule I could tell when they had made love, not from her, because her face was always velvety, luminous, but from him. After sexual intercourse he was pale as a ghost, trembling, as if he had been eviscerated, which was the way he looked now. Hal MacIntyre was very proud of his sexual prowess, of Karen's too, and he was accustomed to tell practically everybody he met that she was the only girl he had ever known who could come any time she wanted to, or any time he wanted her to, an unlimited number of times a day. "I've never met anybody as wonderful as that crazy little Karen," he would mutter with continually amazed satisfaction at her effortless, divine erotic fluency. Yet she gave no impression of eroticism at all; she seemed to be sedate, demure, prudent, with feet on the ground. She never flirted, never paid compliments, and almost always said what she meant, exactly. Of course, Mac never got far away from sex, and he talked incessantly in terms of sexual anecdote and allusion. He was full of odd bits of sexual lore. "If you wear a yellow necktie in France, it means that you're a cuckold," he would say.

We sat at Weber's on the Rue Royale in Paris one autumn afternoon. Karen was around the corner shopping.

"You know how to sleep with one of your wife's servants?" he asked me. "Just get into bed with her. The servant always wants to be one up on the wife."

I thought this was somewhat odious. "Aren't you faithful to Karen?" I asked.

"Yes, but she makes me so mad sometimes I want to go out and fuck a cow." He added, almost angrily, "But it isn't any fun, because I can't tell her about it."

I did not know then that, on a long trip to the Far East the year before, he had got himself blackmailed over a girl in Siam, and that, in Shanghai, he had had a substantial affair, which became widely known up and down the China coast, with a young woman who had been the mistress of one of the uncles of the Emperor of Japan. All during this trip he had written Karen, when he wrote her at all, that he was strictly on the wagon. In fact he had been drunk as a skunk half the time.

We finished our stingers and I said no to another.

"I envy you your drinking habits, Nelson," Mac sighed. "You drink so nicely—in moderation. You drink and don't get drunk." He looked at me with affection, almost enviously. "As for me, I drink because I like to drink. I drink most when I'm happiest. I suppose you would call that strange, that I drink most when I'm happiest. Karen stays right with me too. But I'm not an alcoholic, because the first sign of alcoholism is self-deception, and I've never deceived myself about alcohol or anything else, never in my life. Well, cheers."

I took a good look at him as we sat there—arrogant, with his beautifully shaped head cocked warily, closely cut salt-and-pepper hair, glasses halfway down his nose, long muscular jaw, and blood almost visible in the veins in the temples. Out of doors he almost always wore a soft, shapeless hat crushed far back on the lean head. I had a sudden tangential memory of a scene in London some months before, about which I had never told Karen. Gilmore Scott of the UP, his best friend next to me, took us to lunch in Soho after he had been on a week's binge, and we sought earnestly to perform an impossibility—argue a man out of drinking. Mac was cold, bitterly hostile, and resentful. "So you think I'm a drunkard, do you?" he said icily. He had already had a good deal to drink this day, but he turned to the waiter and ordered a double kirsch with a beer chaser. "No, make that a triple kirsch, please, and I'll have stout instead of beer." He gulped the kirsch and stout and repeated the order. "You sour bastards, you think you can humiliate me by making out that I'm an alcoholic. I'll walk out of this restaurant straighter than either of you." He fell on the floor; we had to drag him to a taxi.

It was, of course, axiomatic that when he was sober he was as delightful as he was offensive when drunk. He told stories beautifully, and he had an easy, friendly, outgoing manner. No correspondent was ever more generous to younger colleagues—giving them a leg up. He was fantastically alert and perspicacious. He wrote leads of classic, crystalline purity and punch. His erudition was considerable, and he understood practically everything worth knowing about contemporary men and politics. He could put odd bits and pieces of news together skillfully, and made stories out of minutiae that almost everybody else missed. When we worked together in the same city, as had recently been the case in London, I called every morning, giving him the outline of the day's news; he hated to get out of bed, and seldom rose before noon. Then lunch with somebody—anybody. He could not bear to eat alone or just with Karen. Over the phone he would sift and winnow the grist I gave him, and he almost always had an idea for an original approach to a story. Sometimes if he had a really bad hangover and Karen couldn't get him up, I would file for him, writing his dispatch and signing it with his name.

Bells clanged through the *Rotterdam,* as a page came up to me with a sheaf of telegrams. I opened them one by one:

KNOWING YOUR LOYALTY JUSTICE RECTITUDE APPEAL YOUR AID RESTORATION MY POSITION

MAXIM LITVINOV

DONT KNOW WHETHER YOU REMEMBER ME BUT PERHAPS YOU MAY RECALL MEETING AT ASTORS STOP APOLOGIZE TELEGRAPHIC ABRUPTNESS BUT MUTUAL FRIENDS ENCOURAGE ME BELIEVE I MIGHT APPEAL YOUR HELP FIND PUBLISHER AND PRODUCER FOR PLAYS I HAVE JUST COMPLETED STOP HEARING YOU LONDON WENT THERE WITH MSS BUT MISSED YOU

BERNARD SHAW

HAVE BEEN URGENTLY REQUESTED INQUIRE OF YOU WHATS HAPPENED TO SQUIRRELS CONFINED HITLERS PANTS KINDLY EXPEDITE ANSWER

SIGMUND FREUD

PURSUANT REQUEST MADAME CHIANG KAISHEK RESPECTFULLY INQUIRE WHETHER POSSIBLE OBTAIN FROM YOU

THE MICROPHONE THROUGH WHICH YOU MADE RECENT RUSSIAN BROADCASTS STOP WILL AUCTION BENEFIT CHINESE REFUGEES

WELLINGTON KOO

JUST ARRIVED LONDON COULD YOU SPARE ME TEN MINUTES

LEON TROTSKY

HAVE EVIDENCE YOU ARE NOT NELSON A NELSON BUT ARE MASQUERADING AS BROADCASTER USING MATERIAL OF WHICH I AM AUTHENTIC AUTHOR STOP WISH HOWEVER YOU AID ME SUPPORT MY CLAIM AGAINST FOUR OTHER IMPOSTORS PURSUING SIMILAR DEVICES

NELSON A NELSON

I did not need to see Mac's broad, aware grin to tell me who had sent these messages. Karen chortled.

The *Rotterdam* gave a cough, and a steward shouted the Dutch equivalent of "All ashore that's goin' ashore."

I have never seen Mac hurry. He was swift, but he never hurried. He finished sipping a third double stinger, and we pushed through the crowd toward the entrance to the gangplank. I stood aside as he kissed Karen good-bye. It was clear that she had something for him that was all, but he would not acknowledge this. "I'll be home in about a month," he said, "if there isn't an invasion." He had a lecture tour coming up. "Take care of Karen, Nelson." To her, with his curious crooked smile, the lips twisted, he smiled, "Be alert. You never know how much I love you."

She always lit his cigarettes for him. There was some delay standing in line, and, as we waited, she popped a cigarette out of her case, lit it with a new lighter I had given them, took a quick puff, and put it between his lips.

I went up to my cabin and finished unpacking. I wouldn't have been able to get on the ship, let alone have a cabin to myself, except for the intervention of the American Embassy in London. I heard the engines grunt; we were getting under way. I took a nap and called Karen in her room a deck below. "What time dinner?" "Around eight," she replied. I felt that she was both pleased and a trifle annoyed to have me so unexpectedly on board; pleased because she liked me, annoyed because—I saw it clearly in her manner—she must have been looking forward, perhaps subconsciously, to a week at sea free of any obligation or commitment, to pick up companions as she willed. She added over the phone, "I may be a minute late. I have to see that the children are settled, and I think Miss M. is going to be seasick any moment." Miss M., their governess, was a stalwart Dane. But it is an absolute rule of life that all governesses, even stalwart Danes, become seasick—as axiomatic as the rule that all illicit love affairs are broken open at last by a misplaced or intercepted letter.

I had seldom seen Karen with her children before. They were well trained, but assertive. She was rather shy about them, almost apologetic, as if they were a mystery to her. "How did these children *happen?* Are they real?" her manner seemed to say. "How can they belong to *me?*"

Waiting for Karen in the smoking room, I amused myself making a list of people I must see in New York. I am the most gregarious of men, blessed by friendship, and I reached twenty names at once. First, of necessity, my bosses at NBS, particularly since I had had it on the grapevine that there was a good deal of opinion in the studio for keeping me on in New York as a kind of foreign editor. For the moment I had forgotten all about Elspeth, who was, of course, the actual reason for my precipitate return.

Karen, looking neat and smart, entered the bar in a dress I had seen several times before—I liked it because the fabric clung to her body, and just above the waist one could see, on close inspection, a tiny protuberance that must be caused by a small mole or something of the sort, making an elevation in the skin, an inverted dimple. We went into dinner and had caviar and steak. She liked beef rare, as did I. We had a bottle of champagne with *crêpes mille-fleurs* and I asked her something and she didn't reply. I asked her the same question again and she said, "Sorry, I wasn't listening." I thought that this was somewhat rude and said so and she apologized. Then, putting her hands over her eyes and pressing the palms in, she exclaimed, "I don't think I can

15

stand it any more. If he doesn't stop drinking, I'll have to leave him."

"What would that do to him?"

"Drive him all the way into the gutter, or be the making of him." She was crying. "Thank God for the children!" Angrily she dabbed her tears away. She was one of those girls, unusual in the modern world, who cried a lot. She was a profoundly emotional person underneath her suave, almost disdainful quality of not giving anything away.

3

It took six days or longer to cross the Atlantic in those dim neolithic times, when men wore BVD's, Lucky Strikes were colored green, and the plural of breast was breast. Presently we met a group of fellow passengers who formed a cluster around our table. Both Mac and I had the knack of being given the best table in a restaurant or similar public place, even if we were not known to the headwaiter. We didn't tip ostentatiously for this privilege; it just happened. Ships were great fun in those days—before the old-style portholes, shaped like collars with a lock, gave way to odiously sealed windows in air-conditioned rooms, before capaciously open decks were chopped up and lit by strips of phosphorescent neon. The *Rotterdam* tossed a bit, rose once or twice on her haunches and banged into the solid white-and-purple water, and provided every amenity for those who played Ping-Pong, lolled in steamer rugs, or walked seven and a half times around the deck to make a mile.

We promised the passengers we met to look them up in New York, London, Hyères, or Munich, in the immemorial manner of ship's passengers, and never —of course—did so. We liked one young woman whose ineffectual-seeming husband was writing a biography of Mussolini; she was miserable, and I was certain that the book would never be finished; she was a typical case of somebody strong being destroyed by someone weak. We liked the New England *grande dame* (born in Ames, Iowa) married to a Hungarian nobleman who had knocked out one of her eyes when he suspected her of infidelity. A smart, snobbish British M.P., who had just lost a by-election by seven votes, was aboard; a Japanese industrialist abnormally tall for a Japanese; and an Englishman dining alone, who never changed for dinner even for the gala, and who was reputed to be a King's Messenger.

The sea became calmer, and the ship creaked gently. One night Karen and I went up to the boat deck, where the lifeboats poised there looked like gigantic pods. I wondered how we, the peas, would ever get into them in the event of an emergency, particularly me with my foot. Any boat drill I have ever seen on a ship has been nonsensical.

Our shoulders touched. Perhaps I imagined it, but I felt that she withdrew half an inch, then pressed close again. I don't think I had ever made a pass at Karen in my life, although, had circumstances been different, I would certainly have wanted to do so. Years before in a pub in Belgrade we had all been drunk and she kicked off her shoes. I reached down and filled one with the red Dalmatian wine we were drinking. She called out, "Hey—stop!" and Mac looked puzzled. Later he scolded me, "That was a damn silly thing to do. Ruining a girl's shoe. What do you think you are—some boulevardier in Lapérouse courting Cleo de Mérode?" Later: "I wouldn't make a pass at your wife. I'd like to, but I couldn't. I'm too fond of you. Don't make a pass at mine." "It wasn't exactly a pass," I replied. The next morning he groaned cheerfully at breakfast, all friction forgotten, saying affably, "I can't *bear* it that you're three years younger than I. Now let's tackle this local ham." Mac loved good food. The Dubrovnik hams were slim as bottles, bright red, and sharp in flavor. We rose to greet Karen. I had my foot then, and we set out to take a walk. Mac said, "I can't bear it that you're two inches taller, either."

His possessiveness toward Karen, his berserk jealousy, even then, was phenomenal, and assumed peculiar forms. Of course nobody can be quite that jealous of a person unless the other wants it so. Karen was not allowed to lunch with any man—even when Mac was absent for months at a time—dine, or, heaven forbid, dance. She was not permitted to laugh in the company of a man. "Laughter is an intimacy—very dangerous!" declared Mac somberly. More startling was his injunction that she must never wear pink, white, or cream-colored underwear, because these reminded him of his first wife, Kathleen. Rather dolefully, Karen had to restrict herself to pale blue, yellow, violet, or, of course, black.

She would fight for him, or their joint interests, like a tigress. I remembered a poker game in Berlin after he had interviewed Hitler for the first time. Extremely drunk, he lost heavily—almost two thousand dollars. He almost never carried money in any amount on his person (he said a wallet gave an unseemly bulge to the pocket) and, with a commanding hangover, set out the next morning to write a check. He could scarcely hold the pen. Karen grabbed the check off the breakfast table and crumpled it in her palm. "Karen," he remonstrated, "you can't do that—this is a debt of honor." "Nonsense," she replied. "You were dead drunk, you couldn't tell one card from another—they kept slipping down into your lap." He made his way out of the house when she was cooking lunch, went to the bank surreptitiously, drew out cash, and paid up.

Now, up on the deck, I put my hand on hers, where it grasped the wet slippery rail. She had lovely slim fingers. Without knowing I was going to say it, I said, "Karen, you're very attractive—just about the most attractive young woman I've ever met."

"Oh, Nels, don't say things like that after all these

years. I might believe them, and you wouldn't like me spoiled."

I leaned over to give her a comradely kiss; she pursed her lips into a small hard unyielding point.

We lurched downstairs, bracing ourselves against the movement of the ship, and she guided me around a steep turn. She had won the ship's pool the day before; now she bid again. She was always one hell of a good gambler.

The tall Japanese came up to us in the lounge, where music was blaring from behind a screen of palms, and invited her to dance. To my astonishment she accepted. The Japanese delivered her back to our table after the dance, bowing. "Don't tell Mac I danced," she breathed to me casually. The Japanese, grinning, hissing, eager to be part of our community, asked archly, "How long you mallied?" "We're not married," Karen said. "At least not to each other. As for me, two years common law, six legal." The Japanese withdrew, bewildered. Yet Karen was only twenty-six, I reflected. I remembered something Mac had said in our salad days. "Catch a girl young—stamp her early. Then she'll never get over you."

4

We were the first big liner to arrive in New York from Europe after the outbreak of the war, and a good deal of confusion and delay occurred at the dock. A naval officer, presumably representing intelligence, searched me out and asked a number of unbelievably naïve questions. I should have paid some attention to helping Karen and the children, but didn't do so; I had to collect my pictures and go through customs. At that time the American customs examination was the most barbaric and exacting in the world. Strips of tape had to be torn off the glass on the paintings to see if there were any nudes among them. I dragged myself down the dock, through a scrimmage of men and women opening trunks (travelers actually did use trunks in those days—I had one myself) and saw friendly faces— Jennifer Noland, my bright young secretary, who had been a Rockette; also my agent, a representative of my sponsor, two or three people from NBS, and, good God, even my old father, who should not have been out of bed. He was a chartered accountant in his seventies, and had arthritis.

I did not see Karen. Well, if any girl could take care of herself, she could.

My memory skipped back momentarily to an event several years before. She had left Berlin for a weekend to join Mac in Brussels, and, safe in their hotel room, said, "Look at this." In her stocking, concealed in the arch of a foot, was a bundle of U.S. dollars. The export of foreign currency was strictly forbidden in the Germany of that day, and smuggling was severely punished; moreover, she had been actually searched in a spot-check at the frontier. A grubby woman took her aside to a cubicle and made her undress completely, but did not inspect her feet with care. If she had been caught, it would have been damaging in the extreme to Mac's public face in Germany, and she herself might have gone to jail. A near thing. Mac was outraged, furious. She smiled snootily. She loved danger.

The next morning I went up to Columbia Presbyterian to have some repair work done on my foot, then wrote the first draft of a big return-from-the-war broadcast scheduled for Sunday. I caught the first plane available, a puddle jumper, to Bangor, and hired a car to reach the backwoods village where Elspeth, who had gone to Maine for a holiday, lay in a rustic hospital. The building was a steep-gabled white cottage with a railed porch, from which the paint was peeling. Her first words were, "What on earth are you doing here?" She was not hostile, but she looked frightened, appraising. "I'm perfectly all right," she groaned, twisting in the narrow bed and then lifting herself to avoid crushing a tube that went somewhere into her body under the bedcovers. "You shouldn't have left your work," she insisted.

"I had just about cleaned it up," I lied. "The war doesn't seem to be moving, and it was time for me to come home."

"Well, darling . . ." she sighed, hugging me. "You look relaxed . . . and I must say I'm glad to see you. You're a pound or two up, aren't you?"

I talked to her doctor, a healthy resolute French Canadian, big in the shoulder, with grizzly iron-colored hair. He had just barely saved her life. The entire peritoneal cavity had been choked with pus. "She was the least cooperative patient I have ever had," Dr. Ralloux stated with good humor. "She must have been in terrible pain, but she resisted the operation to the uttermost." He gave me a long look. "Does she relish pain? Tell me frankly. Does she want to die?"

"I don't think so." I began to feel a marked sense of guilt.

"Well, you must help her to snap out of this mood she's in."

"I'm afraid I've rather neglected her in the past

year or so. She's a difficult person to handle, difficult to live with—critical, sensitive."

"I'll say," replied the doctor. "I know the type. City women who come up here for the summers . . . spoiled—"

"I don't think she's spoiled. She wants too much, but that's something different."

"In any case, I know the type. One layer of skin too few."

A nurse, with her hair in curlers and with big steel-bound glasses, joined us on the porch the next morning. The trees were changing. We were surrounded by trembling scarlet, orange, russet. "Your wife is miraculously better, Mr. Nelson. Seeing you is the best thing that could have happened. My, I never thought I'd actually *meet* you, Mr. Nelson. I follow all your broadcasts. . . ."

There were several secrets to Elspeth, which I do not think that the doctor, for all his superficial insight, could have penetrated on short acquaintance. A major element in her character, aside from her waywardness, was her ability to exert strength through weakness. She looked frail, helpless, bereft, but she was tough as blue jeans underneath. She had a capacity unparalleled in my experience to achieve seemingly impossible results. In other words, she had will. Mac would say roughly, "She's nutty as a fruit-cake," but it was a sane kind of nuttiness—it had direction and produced results. If, as an example, she arrived in London the day of a gala performance at

Covent Garden, sold out for weeks, she could always manage to get a seat in the sixth row on the aisle on an instant's notice. That she was clever as well as infuriating and outrageous was apparent to almost everybody, but not so many people appreciated her durability. With a profusion of golden curls and a slim neck, she looked like a chrysanthemum. Her body was tiny but her head big, atop the stalk of neck. Sometimes she had the appearance of a grand-mother disguised as a child waif. Her thumbs were short, with the nails wide like fans. She liked to make love in odd and improbable places, where, as she put it, she felt the sway of universal motion—in a wheat-field, even in a canoe.

One night we had guests at our old country place near Ridgefield—very conservative people, a sixty-five-year-old diplomat and his starchy wife. On their pillows Elspeth had placed neatly several condoms.

Once I gave her an expensive German camera which, like many cameras in those days, operated with plates or a film pack; the user had to pull a black rectangular slide out of the apparatus between exposures. Elspeth could never remember to pull out this slide, and therefore never got a picture. The symbolism was irritatingly obvious. An obstacle, which she could not learn to remove, blocked her.

We visited one night the apartment in Albany, in London, of a British man of affairs, who had an immense Alsatian growling all over the place. Els-peth said, "Is it male? Could I sleep with it?"

Around a Paris café table a gang of us played a game in which each person was dealt a card on which a question was written; the players had to answer. Elspeth drew "What do you want most in life?" and she wrote down in her faint spidery handwriting, "To have an orgasm every time I am screwed."

Today in Maine she seemed to be in the sunniest of moods. I discussed my next broadcast, and, as always, she had piquant ideas for it. She helped my work a great deal—when I was not too exasperated with her to give her a chance. For years she had been working on and off on a long book—which was to be a large compendium on God, the world, and man in his relation to politics and the universe, with passages of autobiography. But, as she put it, she was a Penelope writer; by night she unwove what she wove by day. Her self-pity about this was maddening. She sucked at me for help like a leech, and when she asked me to reach in the bureau drawer and fetch out a manuscript, to be entitled "My Unlived Life," I quailed. My heart dropped. The section she gave me to read was called "Theo-Politics and Transmission," and seemed to be addressed to me:

Conviction of right message (it) to wrong recipient (Nelson). Depressions are only personal. Optimistic & light hearted for Life, Earth, Space, etc. As always, believing that all is possible, including All the Best. But for me personally, nothing seems possible that I want— my wants are not many but intense—or were so. All were realizable, achievable, & were achieved, made real, lived. But now there's nothing I want that's possible. I've just faced up to that, & it has terrified me. Nothing? said I to myself, can't be nothing, surely not nothing! There must be something, you must want something that's possible. I thought & I thought & I couldn't think of anything, absolutely, in the space-time continuum. . . . I wonder what I'm really afraid of—I've never found out—maybe of Nothing—& what is more fearful than nothing? . . .

We rose to clearer waters. I talked about parties in London, friends in Paris, work, the war, an interview with Litvinov, a weekend on a tawny beach in Estonia, meetings with Daladier and Blum. I had an anecdote about Walter Duranty in Moscow, Bill Stoneman in Rome, and other of our old friends.

"I crossed the Atlantic with Karen MacIntyre," I added.

"The constant nymphomaniac."

My eyebrows lifted.

"And how's your sweetheart—Mac, I mean. How's sharp old drunken Mac?"

Her voice took on an astringent note, and became shrill, discussing Mac and his peccadilloes. "You're much more in love with him than with me," she went on. "It's pure though. Neither of you has a drop of homosexual blood in your veins, I'm glad to say. I suppose, though, that both of you would like to mingle your semen in me."

How astounding, I thought, that anybody so basically proper and correct could be such a bitch. Oh, she could be a mean little woman, Elspeth could!

Of course, she had moments of hating Mac because he had cost me my foot.

"Mac's all right," I said. "At least he was all right a week ago. Keep your fingers crossed."

"You should do more to take *care* of him," Elspeth said, switching from denunciation to solicitude.

"I'm not my sweetheart's keeper."

"How like you to say that. You're never shaken, never stirred. If you pitched in and took sides, you could be a great man. You're too intolerably detached!" But she added after a moment, "You're rock-firm, though, and I like that."

Elspeth, who could not endure criticism, had been thrown off Mac by a single remark he had made when he and Karen had visited us for a weekend in Vienna several Christmases before. It wasn't a political remark, although they had fought doggedly about the Soviet Union, which she talked about as "an economic democracy"; he thought that such an opinion was childish, illiterate nonsense, and said so vehemently. Our cook was out and Elspeth, who is not notably domestic, made dinner, a meatloaf. Mac said quite politely, "Elspeth, you always have delicious food, but these plates are cold." She stared at him as if thunderstruck. The affront was too personal, too piercing. He did not catch this, but he saw that she did not move and he said, "I'll take them out to the kitchen and warm them myself." "You will do no such thing!" she hissed. Karen leaped up and carried the plates out.

I had another talk with the Maine doctor and decided to return to New York that night. Elspeth would be well enough to follow me in a week or two.

Her last words were: "I haven't asked you—what new girls?" Her voice lapsed into a detestable little simper. "What girls are you playing around with now?"

"None," I replied.

5

Mac always said, "Goddamn it, Nels, you work too hard!" and perhaps he was right to a degree, but I am not a grind, and I work swiftly and well rather than merely "hard." God knows I have always taken plenty of time out for pleasure and indulgence. The next day in New York there were two girls I wanted to see, but first I had to do my broadcast on the Polish holocaust. A good deal of emotion went into preparing this. I have several close Polish friends, and for many years the grace, charm, and dignity of Warsaw, together with its elusive note of passion throbbing under the surface, made it one of my favorite cities. I try to be as conscientious as I can in anything having to do with the spoken or written word, and I kept yelling at my secretary, Jennifer, to bring more clips from the library. Midway through my script I had a sudden tangy memory of a Polish girl I had been crazy about a few years before—she nicknamed me "Monsieur Placide."

Whenever I was in New York, I made a kind of festivity out of my weekend broadcasts, and almost always had a guest with me, usually a girl. This had caused a certain amount of trouble with Elspeth, but now she was reconciled to it. In those days I sat before a microphone not in a booth but at a big oval table in a comfortable room, where, listening, my guest or guests would sit. This was taking a chance, because of course any sound made by anybody in the room—a cough, the rustling of a bit of paper, the scraping of a chair—would be picked up by the mike and go out on the air. One night I had a British cabinet minister with me who forgot himself and started to grumble in disagreement at what I was saying; I had to reach for a pencil as I talked, scribble a note, "Shut up!," and shove this to him across the table. Those were the horse-and-buggy days in radio.

New York was, I must interject, an extraordinarily agreeable city to live and work in at this period, and I took delight in rediscovering some of its more obviously pleasurable aspects. The view down Park Avenue toward Grand Central had not yet been ruined by the Pan American monolith, and the tiers of skyscrapers were still made of stone, not glass. There were no erotic movies imported from Scandinavia, and on any number of nights immense crowds filled Times Square waiting for the news.

Nobody had ever seen a TV aerial (although those of us in the communications business knew that TV was coming), and such indignities as a garbage strike or scandals over segregated schools were unknown. It was interesting to notice that most traffic cops were fat—never in London or Paris did one see a fat cop—and that live steam poured out of manhole covers in the street. I could not get over the fantastic noisiness of the city after the tranquillity and silence, comparatively speaking, of most European capitals. Here police sirens, fire bells, whistles, mechanical shrieks and screams, assailed the ears beyond measure, and the nostrils quivered at the stink of burning rubber as cars wheeled and swooped down tawdry streets. In comparison with today, New York in the virginal thirties was a group of small towns loosely strung together. It had not yet become a smothering megalopolis; it was not too difficult to be leisurely, traffic had not become throttling, and the city had little-known byways still fascinating to explore.

Karen MacIntyre sat with me this night, and after my show and after taking a few phone calls from nuts, or addicts, we coasted down the street to "21." Walking a block or two was not too difficult if I went slowly. It was a calm evening, with a thin slice of moon. We were welcomed pleasantly into "21," and I gave her the news of Elspeth.

"Does she ever come to your broadcasts?" Karen asked.

"No, and I'm glad she doesn't. She'd make me go

through the roof with nervousness. But she listens carefully, and often has useful things to say."

"Sometimes I think it would be the best thing in the world for both of you to give her a good sound kick in the pants."

"I'm bound to her," said I.

"I suppose you're still in love with her."

"No, not that. It's a different kind of bondage. I'm fond of her and I feel that I have to take care of her—perhaps out of some obscure sense of guilt."

"You're just an old softie, Nels, but very dear."

"What word from Mac?" I asked.

"He seldom writes, but I get a cable every once in a while. But this time he hasn't acknowledged my cable announcing our safe arrival. Mostly I keep up with him by watching the paper for his dispatches."

So did I. There hadn't been anything for a day or two. Karl, my favorite waiter, in his bright red jacket, awaited us attentively and we ordered jellied borscht and two brizzolas, on the bone.

I felt my affection for Karen glow and grow. Her hair was so soft that, wearing it a new way, she couldn't comb it with precision; the part was crooked. We were sitting side by side on a banquette, and several times during dinner, when our hips happened to touch, she moved an inch or so away, as if she didn't want to risk being too close.

"I had lunch today with Aaron Rafael. He's surprised you haven't phoned him," Karen said with our coffee.

Aaron was my lawyer, the MacIntyres' lawyer too. He was a small man, bald, with sloping shoulders and sensitive, inviting hands. Karen called him a *Gneisser*, a taster. He had five children, all girls, between the ages of two and nine.

"He's so sad, so lonely," Karen said. "Still chases every girl he meets, in spite of that huge family."

"From bed to worse," I quipped.

"I like him because nothing ever puts him off. He's undimmable, unquenchable. He's been in love with me for years—I mean it—seriously."

This remark, casually stated as it was, affected me profoundly. I look back to it now, as a matter of fact, as one of the turning points of my life. Karen never talked loosely about anything, and I perforce had to accept what she said as a hard fact. But it turned my world topsy-turvy. Karen belonged to Mac, Mac to Karen. That any outsider should penetrate their sacred precincts was unthinkable; no incursions from exterior realms could be permitted here. But now Karen was affirming clearly that somebody—a friend who was also a friend of *mine*—had the temerity, the wanton push and pull, to be *in love with her*. I gasped, as it dawned on me that Aaron Rafael had broken the taboo, an extraordinarily serious taboo. He was in love with Karen and she knew it. In a peculiar way this opened her to me. She was freed.

"You haven't had an affair with him?"

"Of course not. Good Lord, no!"

She caught something of the intense emotion I was feeling, and looked up, concerned and puzzled.

We made our way down the street to Fifth Avenue, and the moon had developed more substance and a little color. I held her forearm tight—it was round, firm, youthful, warm. Naturally we went to the Stork Club, the inevitable next stop in those days on this particular circuit. A heavy-set headwaiter who had to shave two or three times a day lifted the rope and we entered the Cub Room, shaped like an amoeba. In a moment a bottle of champagne appeared at our table, compliments of the omniscient, all-seeing, and proficient management. To be a celebrity—albeit an extremely minor celebrity in this milieu, with stars scattered about in profusion—was, I thought, somewhat vulgar but satisfying too. There were nods from table to table, and kibitzers wandered in and out.

The band in the next room played something I liked. Of course I couldn't dance, but it was pleasant watching other people make these preposterous turns and shakes and bends. Karen was quite good—intuitive to rhythm, supple, a girl who completely molded herself to her partner with grace and a nice note of submission to command. But she wasn't a patch on Mac, who it just happened was one of the best ballroom dancers any of us had ever met.

We drank some more champagne. No longer did I feel like Monsieur Placide. I thought of the long years of our friendship, but this night something magical, bewitching, gave it a different focus. I saw her as a romantic and intensely desirable entity of her own, not merely as a comradely adjunct to Mac. She, too, seemed to be expressing a new warmth toward me, a new curiosity and loving interest.

Karen said abruptly, "Let's go. I feel lewd, and loose, and bawdy."

I took stock for a split second. "I don't like the thought of a hotel."

"My place isn't possible," Karen said. "I'm in a single room at the Lafayette, and they know Mac too well. Besides, the children are in the room next door."

I sought to be very calm. "We could go to my apartment, but I have a servant there, old Ogda."

"We don't have to wake her up, do we?"

6

Karen had to go to Denver, Mac's home town, the
next day, because arrangements had been made for
her to stay there with the children, living with the
MacIntyre family, until Mac returned to the United
States. Mac's father was a surgeon—extremely conservative, I gathered, with a long-established and
successful practice. Mac had three brothers and one
sister, scattered nearby, all with growing families.
The clan had an adhesive family sense, conventional
but strong religious convictions (they were Method-
ists, I believe), and lusty sexual patterns. The old
doctor, Karen told me, still demanded satisfaction
from his aged and enfeebled wife every day, although he was in his seventies. "Even for this day
and age," she muttered grimly on one occasion, "that
family is oversexed!"

Then she reconsidered, "As a matter of fact, you

can't be *over*sexed, can you? You're just sexed, or under." I replied, "I'm under, thank goodness. Saves me a lot of trouble." She threw a napkin at me, making a grimace.

I met one of Mac's brothers in Europe once, and was astonished to hear him call Mac "Ralph." Indeed, that was his name, but he was never anything but "Mac" to us, although Karen sometimes used a childhood nickname, "Hal." I discovered, too, that this brother hated Mac, because he was so "overbearing."

I drove Karen, the two children, and their nurse out to LaGuardia in an NBS limousine. The night before had been the most profound as well as delicious and enthralling experience I had ever had. At first I was numb with inhibition. I had visions of Elspeth, having risen miraculously from her hospital bed and flown to New York, sailing into the room without warning, a menacing angel in a black cloud. And I felt blurred by other worries. I was gripped by bad conscience about Mac. With tenderness and skill, Karen, who showed no signs of guilt at all, rid me of my shortcomings. The experience was more radiantly satisfying and complete than anything I had ever known. I remembered Mac's talk about her effortless, passionate fluency and capacity for infinite response. "I never knew I'd feel so much *emotion!*" Karen cried trembling when a strip of dawn became luminous on a windowsill. Now driving to the airport, with conversation impossible because of the children, she still had an exalted, almost reverent look.

I kissed her on the cheek and murmured something as she boarded the plane. She controlled herself, chitchatted a moment, and then said with her wide, level smile, giving me *congé,* "Don't lead a clean life, but be clean."

*

Ten days later I brought Elspeth back to town—a length of stubby tube, like a spigot, still projected from her body. I did not write Karen, nor did I hear from her for about a month. Then came a brief letter, informing me that Mac was arriving in New York the next week, and that she was thinking of coming east to meet him. The letter was cool as crystal, but conveyed much. It called for a reply, and clearly I had three alternative choices of action. I could deliberately not answer, but wait for the telephone call that would surely come when she arrived. Or I could write to say categorically but with delicacy that what had happened between us should not happen again. Or I could welcome her with delight, hoping that we would ardently resume our affair. When finally I had worked out what I wanted to say, after two or three false drafts, and sealed the envelope, I waited a long moment at the mail chute before dropping it in. I knew with absolute conviction that I was taking one of the major decisions of my life, one of incalculable permanent importance. I was nailing down my own future; perhaps casting a doom upon myself. There was a harsh clarity to this conviction of inevitability beyond my power to describe. This was a genuine salute to the point of no return. I dropped the letter in.

I met her train at Grand Central, and took her to the St. Regis, where a small suite had been reserved for Mac by his office. I watched her unpack—so neat, so deft—and thought in contrast of the way Elspeth packed and unpacked, a phenomenon that resembled a tempest blowing through an underwater cave. We had lunch at Maud's on Forty-ninth Street, a glossy little restaurant I liked, and I said after coffee, "No broadcast today, I'm free all afternoon. Would you like to see Garbo in *Ninotchka?*"

She gave me a look as if to say that I must have lost my mind. "Nelson, are you being shy, obtuse, Scandinavian, or don't you want me any more?"

We drove to the hotel. We held hands tightly in the taxi, and I kissed her. "You shouldn't kiss like that except in bed," Karen said.

In the bedroom at the St. Regis we both had our clothes off in seconds. The room had a tall, old-fashioned, carved white commode with three full-length mirrors; in these our images rippled and coalesced. Years later I would remember that afternoon, every aspect of it, the topaz dusk gradually filling the room, the suffusion of amber, violet, rose, lurking in the curtains, as well as every detail of Karen's talk and behavior, her unceasing flow and urgency, every nuance and delicate shift in an embrace.

"I'm so glad it's a beautiful room," Karen said, her voice low, her face luminous. "Do you feel the pain I feel, a sweet pain—near the heart?"

"I don't feel anything but the purest distillate of pleasure."

"That's impossible. You must feel some small sense of guilt as well. I do, at least. I didn't the first time, but I do now. Maybe that's because it's more important now. Believe it or not, I love my husband. But when I want something, I *want* it. I suppose I'll get over you in time, but I don't want to."

"I certainly don't want you to."

"Oh, darling! I'm so frightened of myself and what I feel for you. This is the first time I've been really happy in a year. Why do you go after girls so much?"

"I didn't used to. An opinion at fifty dollars an hour from a psychiatrist might be that it's compensation for my foot."

"From now on you won't need anybody except me."

"Take that off," Karen commanded, after we had had a sandwich. Of course I had removed the shoe from my bad foot, but the artificial apparatus was still there.

"What do you do with it ordinarily when you go to bed?"

"Toss it in a corner."

She took it off and kissed the stump.

7

Dreamily, drowsily, we talked, dozed, made love, and had a drink.

"What do you like most in the world?" she whispered.

"This. You."

"What else?"

I stretched. "The scent of limes, good roomy closets, footnotes, sunshine on lake water, Aldous Huxley, *pommes Anna*."

"That's a slightly pretentious list, my fine friend. Unsensual, too. Hate most?"

"Wire coat hangers."

She laughed. "Mac has more than thirty suits, including tweed jackets. All from Anderson & Sheppard, too. How many suits have you got, Nelson?"

"About six, I suppose."

"I must say you always look like a bedroll. I

remember, though, that time in Brussels when you appeared in a gray stripe that was identical with something Mac had bought a year before. I thought that was carrying idolatry—" she smiled—"a little far. But it made me care for you more."

"What do you like best?" I asked.

"To have my back held. Has Mac ever been unfaithful to me, do you know?"

"I don't think so," I lied.

"It would be silly of him, wouldn't it? He says I'm better than any whore."

She was striding around the room stark-naked, something she loved to do.

"I don't think that being good at it or not has much to do with infidelity. That comes mostly for emotional reasons, doesn't it?"

"Why do you suppose I'm doing this with you, now? Believe me, I am not a promiscuous woman, and I had an extremely puritanical upbringing. I thought menstruation was a punishment for masturbation. I'll never forget happening to catch a glimpse of my mother and father making love when I was about ten. They always put on the most conventional, proper, puritanical front. And there they were doing *soixante-neuf.*"

"I hope you didn't call the police. Have you ever had anybody but Mac and, now, me?"

"There was a boy before Mac, in Minneapolis, when I was only seventeen, before I went to Berlin.

Mac doesn't know—good Lord, don't ever tell him, it would kill him. He *has* to think he was the first."

"Nobody else?"

"Not until you, darling." She squirmed in bed. "Mac taught me everything I know. He was the first interesting man I ever met. He made me an adult. He created me. He was gentle in those days, patient, considerate, even when I was nothing more than a plaything, and, underneath that inferiority, he was full of *élan*—gay, buoyant, although Kathleen, that bitch, hurt him terribly. Isn't it strange—I still want him to be *madly* in love with me. And he taught me about love and making love—I'll be everlastingly grateful to him for that. But for years I thought he had no guts, because he wouldn't divorce Kathleen— he was afraid of hurting her. I've always wanted him to be happy more than me. . . . Of course he *is* me. Well, it seems to have come out all right, more or less. When we got married at last, I remember saying to myself, actually as the service was going on, 'Yesterday I was nothing. Today I'm Mrs. Ralph MacIntyre!' "

"Did he drink so much in those days?"

"Yes, but it never seemed to be a problem. The problem was to get him to realize that his tutelage was working, that I was growing too. He *still* thinks basically that I'm a kind of child who's fun in bed."

"He's right on that, all right." I wished I could think of something brighter to say.

"He's eleven years older, and I have to be his

45

mother, companion, secretary, and nurse—really, it's too much!" Again she turned in bed, making me stir out of my drowsiness. "But I love him, I'll always love him, and you mustn't ever try to take that away, Nelson!"

I lay on my back, she astride me, myself within her. "Oh, good, darling, so good," she murmured. . . . "Short," she added with the voice of a connoisseur, when we had finished, "but so good, oh, darling, good!" Still astride me, myself still within her, she reached for the telephone. I thought of Elspeth, tense and soundless during the act of love, in contrast to Karen with her low moans, whispers, murmurs, exhalations of delight. Karen said, "I really must let Aaron know that I'm in town—Mac would think it was queer if I didn't call him." She had rather bad telephone manners, since she regarded the telephone as an instrument of communication rather than of conversation; this, too, was a contrast to Elspeth, who like to talk on the telephone for hours. When Karen was finished with Aaron, I disengaged myself and reached for the phone too, calling Elspeth.

"How are you, sweet? Yes, just clearing things up at the office. Is there any food in the house? Karen MacIntyre just dropped into town, and I thought I'd bring her home to dinner."

We drove uptown. At the door Karen touched my arm. "Darling, be careful not to act too happy."

*

46

In those days Elspeth and I lived in a somewhat extravagant apartment on Central Park West overlooking the reservoir, and this view gave her enchantment day and night. The rooms had floors burnished and glistening like trout streams, with a few Moroccan and Persian rugs placed here and there. The walls of the living room and dining room were pale green, and immense off-white sofas, like oblong balloons, were splashed with just the right number of harlequin cushions in a darker green, orange, and bright blue. The furniture was mostly Spanish—large dark walnut chairs and tables, with the appropriate slim ironwork, which I had picked up in Madrid a few years before. The paintings I had brought home on the *Rotterdam* shone marvelously on the pale green walls.

Ogda had prepared a handsome *blanquette de veau* with a spinach salad, and after dinner we played some imported Vivaldi records and then some Memphis jazz, and began to talk about Mac. I recalled the time he had set out to fly the Atlantic westward in an old Junkers crate, a biplane practically held together by pieces of string—as a stunt for his newspaper, very dangerous. Luckily the plane lost an engine and had to turn back to Bremen before it was well over the North Sea. It would certainly never have succeeded in crossing the Atlantic, but Mac was game enough to take the chance.

Then, too, I mentioned the time he had a quarrel with Dr. Goebbels at a *Bierabend* in Berlin, and had snapped at him, "Herr Doktor, you can kiss my ass." He paused, came closer, and added, "Now that I see your face more clearly, I withdraw the offer."

Not long after, Mac, Karen, and I had spent a weekend at Bray on the Thames, where the local inn was celebrated for its good cooking, and I took a sheaf of photographs of him with a new camera—big close-ups of his face. These I mounted on postcards, each with a comedy identification—"Mac at Rest," "Mac Preparing to Tell Off the Boss," "Mac in Dudgeon," et cetera. How we all laughed!

"Oh, he *loves* you," Karen said.

She said she was tired and went home early. I walked her to the door of the elevator, but I did not think that I ought to take her home, although I was wild to make love to her again. Then she paid me a compliment which made me reel with delight: "You're good, you're generous, you're kind." It did not even occur to me that I might have been more pleased if she had used adjectives more exciting.

Elspeth said after she left, "It can't be denied, she's a lovely girl. And she always looks as if she had just been bedding with a man, so well laid."

I had my nose in a book.

8

Mac was returning to the United States by air, which was still a somewhat unusual thing to do in those days; regular service across the Atlantic by the old Clippers—seaplanes—had only begun that summer. The American correspondents still in Europe hated their advent, because it meant that a lot of copy previously cabled could go by airmail, and all correspondents hate mailers except possibly me. Once, working for the UP, I set a record that stood for years—I wrote eleven mailers in a day.

There came a spell of bad weather in the Azores, with a six-foot swell; Mac was stuck there for day after day, and I could imagine his explosive mood.

I kissed Karen. "Aren't we taking an awful chance?" I asked her in the dim light of the small, pretty hotel room. "He might just pop in at any minute."

"No, I call Pan American twice a day, and they've promised to let me know the minute the plane takes off. Besides, there's another stop, in Bermuda."

I thought about it.

"Are you afraid of Mac?" she asked me.

"No."

"He'd kill you. I mean it, *kill* you."

"I don't think he would, but I certainly hope he doesn't find out." I smiled. "You don't talk in your sleep, do you?"

"No. Not yet."

I had the provisional thought that deep down in her heart she wanted to be free of him but that she must be innocent of any act or contrivance that might lead to this end. She shrank from the responsibility for his possible destruction. I changed my mind. No, no. Not for anything would she ever leave him. What might happen to me, whether my life would be ruined or not, did not matter in the least. This was a hard fact to face and bear, because by this time I was violently, uncontrollably in love with Karen MacIntyre. She throbbed in me, literally, from morning to night. I felt that I was riding a whirlwind. I lived in a glowing blur. The intensity and completion of my emotion were particularly astonishing to me because I had never felt anything like it before. Nor had I ever been made so much of before. I have always, unlike Mac, been rather diffident about my prowess. Sure, I went after girls, but I have never felt that I was attractive to women, which was another reason why Karen enraptured me. I did not think I was a good lover at all, and yet she found me satisfying.

"Dearest, turn a little. I think you fibbed to me the other day. *Has* Mac ever been untrue to me?"

What the hell, I thought. Out with a little of it. I said carefully, "He told me once that he had had an affair with a girl in Siam."

The effect on her was startling, and I could have cut my tongue out. Her head wobbled, as if the bones of her neck had been broken, and she flung herself on the floor, face down, crying angrily. She rubbed her cheeks against the carpet as if flagellating herself.

"It must have been because a Siamese girl belongs to a different *race*. He must have been curious, that's all."

I could have said a good deal more. A year or so before, he had called me in Berlin, asking me to rush over to a small hotel on a side street off Kurfürsten-damm, where he was waiting in the lobby. He gleamed with joviality and satisfaction. "Go upstairs," Mac said, giving me a room number. "There's a girl there, American, about twenty-three, a journalism student, quite good-looking. I've just had her. Now I've fixed it for you, and she expects you. I want you to try her out, tell me what you think."

This was not an experience I found edifying in retrospect.

"Maybe we should make a clean breast of it when

Mac returns," I said, contradicting what I had said before. "I don't like this situation."

"I don't like it either, but, my dear, I don't see what a clean breast would do, except cause tragedy. I don't want to leave Mac—I *couldn't* leave Mac!" Her face took on an irritated, helpless look.

"A dilemma," I said, briefly.

"Then there's Elspeth to think about, if you ever give her a thought, which I doubt if you do. You don't want to leave Elspeth, do you?"

"No, even though she's like holding a hedgehog."

"Well, then. There's no solution but to accept it as a triangle in the French way, but secret."

"A quadrangle. And this is America, not France."

"Well, anyway, I'll never be one of those dreadful women who make trouble for a man," she said with rebellious determination. "Dearest, I must ask you to be careful not to muss my hair, because I have to leave in an hour to have a drink with Aaron."

We lay back, clinging skin to skin, consumed, exhausted, enraptured, after the heavenly urgent clamor, the throbbing beat, and the room spun around to rest. She patted her warm flat tummy, saying dreamily, "Good strong babies come out of there. Oh! You should see the way I have babies!"

"Not one just now, I hope."

"Of course I get pregnant if you talk to me on the telephone."

She drifted into talk of Mac, as she almost always did after we made love. I wanted to make love again, but her mood was otherwise, and she pushed me away after a little wrestling. I persisted. "Oh, go and put some cold water on it," Karen said. I had to laugh, and she laughed too.

*

Mac's laziness, forgetfulness, lack of consideration for her, and cranky selfishness in general had increased out of hand in the past year or so, she told me. She gave vent to various small fed-upnesses and irritations. He lolled in bed, dozed or slept ten, twelve hours a day, she said, and nothing seemed to interest him except when he would have enough money to retire, which he proposed to do in Peking. He had been offered fifteen hundred dollars from an American magazine for an article on Goering, which he could have written in half a day, but he never wrote it. He never answered a letter—he had not even acknowledged the communication telling him that he had won a Pulitzer prize. He could seldom remember details of any political talk after midnight; he had managed some months before to get a long interview with Dr. Schacht, after a long period of waiting; then he could not remember accurately anything that Schacht had said. His hypochondria had become acute, together with an instinct for self-pity and glorification. As to his temperament—my God!

Once, when they still lived abroad, he had run down to Toulon alone for a week's passage in the sun, whereupon Karen received a frantic telegram to meet him at the Gare de Lyon in Paris with money and an ambulance to take him to the American Hospital at once; he had been mugged and rolled, and was the victim of a violent ear infection. It turned out that his money was quite intact—crumpled in a knot in an overcoat pocket—and that the ear infection was nothing more than an innocent plug of wax.

Ah, but there were other memories! Once in a Berlin café he had left her for a moment or two to go to the men's room; while he was out of the hall a man at an adjacent table made a pass as her. She was white and shaking when Mac returned. "Which man was it?" Mac demanded sternly, as she described the episode. She pointed him out; Mac strode over, yanked at the man, and socked him. It was the wrong man. What a commotion! I had an anecdote to match. Mac and I sat in the Oak Room in the Plaza in New York, close to the entrance door. A drunken beggar, a bum off the streets, staggered in. The headwaiter started pushing him out, with other waiters helping. Mac rose and tackled the headwaiter, who crashed to the floor. His automatic instinct was to defend the intruding bum, not the establishment.

Karen told me how, when she was returning to England from a brief visit to Paris, he had crossed from Dover to Calais to meet her, and then led her into a *stateroom* he had engaged for the hour's return voyage. He couldn't wait.

He loved Karen, but what he really wanted, he

told me once, was to be rich enough to be able to maintain fully functioning establishments in four different cities—London, Berlin, Rome, New York—with a permanent mistress in each. I asked him once, "What do you want most?" and he replied somewhat pompously, "To do as little work for as much money as possible." He saw my somewhat disapproving look, and snapped, "That's a straight answer—I'm not a hypocrite."

One evening in Paris I invited him to what I said would be the best dinner the city could provide. "How much are you prepared to spend?" he asked cagily. "One hundred dollars," I replied. With delight we worked out a menu that would cost exactly a hundred dollars, not a franc more or less. Our preparations were grandiose and elaborate. When we reached the restaurant, Mac said that the sommelier had insulted him, and he refused to eat a morsel of anything. *How* spoiled could a man get? But I continued to be fascinated by him and loved him.

It was Mac who, six or seven years before, had dared to break open the story of the Reichstag Fire, which brought Hitler to power—exposing it as a Nazi frame-up. And, more than any other correspondent, he explored and wrote about the outrages of the Nazi terror. Day by day he cabled chapter-and-verse accounts of Jews being beaten up and other outrages against the Jewish community. This was an extremely dangerous as well as courageous and upright thing to do. He might well have been murdered by the Nazi gangsters. Not only did he seriously imperil his professional position within Germany by these stories, becoming a public enemy in the eyes of the Nazi regime, but he risked his job at home, where he was undiscriminatingly attacked as a sensationalist and rumormonger by ignorant or biased elements in the local opinion. There were many Americans in those days too innocent to believe that such atrocities could occur in a presumably civilized country like Germany, or too committed to not-rocking-the-boat and holding to a "You-Can-Do-Business-With-Hitler" line. The weasel-hearted in New York went after Mac hammer and tongs. He almost lost his job.

A consequence of this was that Hal MacIntyre became a hero to Jews all over the world, particularly to those who fled from Germany in this period. When Mac himself left Berlin and moved to Paris, his doorbell on the Quai Bethune would ring hour after hour, day after day, and there would appear some bereft, penniless Jewish refugee from the Nazi horror who would stand helplessly at the door, asking for advice or just plain begging. After some months he could no longer bear to see these victims of cosmic catastrophe face to face. He could not endure the note of irremediable lostness in their tormented eyes. So he set up an indirect relief system through the concierge. Any Jewish refugee from the Nazis who could prove any association with Mr. MacIntyre would be given a thousand francs, at that time about twenty dollars, on condition that Mr. MacIntyre himself didn't have to see him.

Presently Mac reached Bermuda, but there the weather closed in on him again. Karen and I waited with impatience, and I said wearily one afternoon, sitting with her in the hotel, "When he does come back, all this between us ends, of course."

"It can't end," she replied. "There's too much between us now. Another thing—I can't get used to not fighting every minute. When Mac comes back, I'll miss my cues."

"But after all we'll be living in different cities. I don't imagine we'll be able to meet often, at least not right away."

"I can't give you up," Karen said. "My life simply isn't worth living if you don't have some share in it."

"Well, we'll see how things come out."

"If only I didn't think of you *all* the time!"

"What would happen if I fell in love with someone else?" I asked.

"All my hormones would be aroused, and I'd pursue you to the ends of the earth. Ah, darling, I adore you, take me, take me."

"Sometimes I think it's rather extraordinary that both Mac and I have this same feeling of intensity about you."

She looked modest, baffled. "I suppose . . . I don't know what . . . there must be *some*thing in me."

We worked out a system for mail, and invented a

false name for her. She would pick up letters at General Delivery in Denver once a week. I shivered a little at such overt duplicity.

I arrived home that evening after a broadcast about affairs in the Middle East, and Elspeth said that I looked tired. The telephone rang and I jumped to it and heard Karen's taut, level voice.

"He's arrived. Dead drunk."

9

I did not want to call them, but I came near to blowing up from the strain of not hearing from her. At the end of the second day Mac telephoned me. "I'm lecturing at Town Hall tomorrow morning at eleven. Let's have lunch later."

His lecture was spirited, competent, and deeply felt—a plea for the United States to enter the war at once in support of the British and French. At lunch he showed no signs at all of having been drinking, but his manner was a little too crisp, too short. Karen seemed to be as calm as a turtle, but she told me later that she had been fairly twitching with nerves. Mac paid no attention to her, but directed all his talk to me. He encased her, so to speak. Almost always when they were together, he behaved as if she had no free will or mind of her own; indeed, he gave her room for little.

Mac gave it as his considered opinion (and this was in October, 1939, remember) that the United States would enter the war within months. Of course this was because he wanted it so much. The intensity of his own desire warped his judgment out of all reasonable limits. He was much too ardent, too much given to the wish as father to the thought. I said that I thought he was gravely underestimating the force and pervasiveness of isolationist sentiment in this country, that it might be a long, long time before we entered the war, and that quite possibly we would not be brought into it at all unless we were provoked by some fluke or extrinsic incident, like an attempt by Hitler to bomb New York. Mac stared at me as if I were bereft of my senses. He stated, "But it is absolutely essential to our national honor and destiny, to say nothing of our basic self-interest, to enter the war at once!" I replied, "Wait and see." He snarled at me, "But are you treasonable? Are you a poltroon?" Trying not to lose my temper, I replied, "Shut up, Mac. You haven't got the picture yet." He spat out, "You're influenced by your crazy wife, a pacifist!" "No," I replied. He added with reckless megalomania, "I myself will bring the United States into the war!"

"By lecturing? You won't reach more than ten thousand people in six weeks."

"My audiences are to be measured by their qualitative merit, not quantitative."

He was so angry that I thought he would hit me. I

did not mention that I reached about twenty million people every weekend.

"Goddamn it, Nelson, you talk like Lindbergh!"

"I certainly do nothing of the kind."

"That's about enough, boys," Karen said.

I remembered swiftly another time years before when he had been very angry, in Berlin, before their marriage. We were dining at Horcher's; he loved sumptuous food and adored Horcher's, where he was a kind of pet. He ordered the caviar inside the baked potato, a specialty of the house which was unknown elsewhere at the time, and Karen made a somewhat uxorious remark about how expensive it was. He snapped at her, "Don't behave like a wife!" In humiliation and fury, she left the table and stamped out of the restaurant. "Mac, you oughtn't to yell at Karen like that," I protested. He grunted at me that it was none of my business, adding, "She'll be back." Indeed, she returned in half an hour, having cooled off in a nearby café. Perhaps his behavior was excusable because, if I remember correctly, he was just at this time getting a divorce from Kathleen, and wifery in any form was a subject that made all his antennae quiver.

Now, today, this day, a million miles removed in space and time, we said brisk farewells in front of Tony's, and I clambered into a taxi to get back to work. They were setting out on a long lecture tour the next day. Not merely did Karen have to accompany him, but she had to attend every lecture, each one identical, some thirty-five in all. That it might bore her to hear the same hour's talk thirty-five times never occurred to him. In regard to the physical strain involved, he said merely that she was eleven years his junior and if he could take it she could. Such a tour, as everybody came to know later, made extraordinarily crippling demands. The scurry to catch the train, the stolen disturbed naps in parlor cars, the yap-yap of the female guests assembled at the lecture hall, the unending dinners with overdone lamb chops and noisome little stone-hard peas, the scampering hordes of autograph seekers, the vapid local celebrity in the front row of the audience who, after every lecture, asked questions already answered, the dreary overheated hotels with their long, moth-eaten, dusty corridors, the horror cities in the South where liquor was available only in the form of "packaged goods" that had to be bought in shops, and the portly, face-lifted women with their hair just out of ironmongery who constituted the glue of every audience—my God, those women! Mac ate all this up. To Karen it was unadulterated agony, but Mac was flattered, stimulated, and revivified.

Thirty-five times she heard him tell the little joke about the Chinese sundial and its inscription, "It is later than you think"; thirty-five times she listened to his reverent account of his first meeting with Mr. Churchill and the way Churchill had rehearsed his remark about Russia being a puzzle wrapped in a mystery inside an enigma.

I could not wrest my mind free from Karen after their departure. Nothing else had any reality at all. She had become indissolubly part of me, bone of my bone. Of course, there was my friend, work, as an anesthetic. My rating held steady, and I was given new and better quarters at NBS. I lunched out a good deal in a set new to me—rich women, archers after celebrities, who made up what came to be called Café Society. I was summoned to Washington, met President Roosevelt for the first time, and was much impressed by his characteristics of infinite skill, style, and balance. Then at a party I ran into a dark lovely girl, Brazilian, with eyes the shape and color of olives, carrying discernment and wisdom far beyond her years, which were only twenty, and with long beautiful hands that might have been made of soft ivory. She became my adored confidante, and I still love her and see her occasionally—bless her!

Elspeth and I had a *modus vivendi* about this sort of thing. She felt that my flirtatiousness was mild enough, innocent enough, and might be indulged in within reason. Our arrangement, largely unspoken and undefined, was that I was free to do anything I wanted at lunch and in the afternoon, but that dinner and evenings were strictly reserved for home. I was not permitted to take anybody out to dinner, but I did not mind this stricture much. I found it rewarding to read at home in the evenings, and there were plenty of dinner parties, to many of which I went alone because Elspeth didn't want to go; she hated to leave the apartment at night except occasionally to see a show.

One afternoon I arrived home early and found there our doctor, Harrison Crocker, who was giving Elspeth a final check-up. We had been the closest of friends for years. Crocker was intellectually tough, physically gentle, with a broken nose, carefully clipped mustache, and spaniel's eyes. He had all manner of outside interests—collected pipes, played the cello and other instruments, sailed a boat. He always said he knew nothing about dermatology because this had been an 8 A.M. course at medical school and he had never been able to get to class, since he played the tuba in a night club to pay his way through school, which kept him up all night. He certainly knew a great deal about everything else.

Harry pronounced Elspeth O.K.

She said, "Have a look at Nelson. He's been having nightmares."

"Oh? What have you been up to?"

"Nothing much."

"Nightmares are caused by roast goose, pickled meatballs, emotional suffocation, or bad conscience."

"We don't have roast goose or pickled meatballs," Elspeth said.

"Well, relax. You look tense, for you," he said to me.

"I'm relaxed enough, but I do have a lot of problems in the studio."

"I know. But here, I'll give you a prescription for some phenobarb. Take it easy."

One night around this time I announced to my audience that I was not a broadcaster, but a narrow-caster. This was not much of a joke, but I was trying to project the idea that all the serious commentators on the air—Murrow, Swing, Davis, Kaltenborn, Sevareid—were no longer content merely to give a broad woolly conspectus of the news at large but sought to concentrate instead on the inner meaning of events—"depth journalism" (loathsome phrase), as it came to be called much later. One thing that worried all of us who were conscientious was the incalculable, prodigious power we commanded not only because of the enormousness of our audiences but because of the nature of the medium. A twist in intonation, a slant in the emphasis on a word, could make the most innocuous statement sensational or provocative. And all of us—good friends, good colleagues—worked together to improve our standards. Journalism is the only profession I know where the keenest rivals are often the best of friends.

A few evenings after the talk with Crocker, Elspeth and I went to see *Abe Lincoln in Illinois*, her first evening out since her illness. Arriving home, she went straight to bed, while I dawdled with a beer. I leafed through some magazines newly arrived from England, and glanced for half an hour into a novel by somebody named Sillanpää, a Finn or Icelander whom nobody had ever heard of, but who had just won a Nobel prize. I clomped down the corridor to our bedroom and saw that the light on my bed table was on, though Elspeth had curled herself into a circle almost like a doughnut, and was sound asleep. Pinned to my pillow by a brooch was a note in her spidery handwriting: "Screw Me Twice Tonight."

*

I tried to analyze my thoughts about Elspeth and sought—once more!—to lay out neatly the complicated strands of her character. She was a true original, no doubt about that, but why in that case did I find her so intolerably boring? It must be because she was so difficult. Perhaps that was the key word, "difficult." She performed even such a routine function as getting dressed as if she were a bird building a nest. Her speech was curious; she had the mannerism of enunciating every word with care, ringing her lips around the vowels. She continually sought my improvement—made me listen to Scarlatti, made me read about Delacroix. She was the kind of girl who, on her first stroll on a lawn, would inevitably find a four-leaf clover. Never once since we had settled into Central Park West had she been to our neighborhood grocery store, butcher, delicatessen, or hardware shop—not once! She left everything to Ogda, or did it on the telephone.

There was scarcely a day during this particular period when we did not have visitors, and they thronged through our apartment every afternoon.

When traveling I met, of course, hundreds of people, and I always asked them to look us up when they passed through New York. Alas, many did. The strain was greater on Elspeth than on me, although it was I, as a rule, who ordered the necessary cocktail stuff, superintended the arrangements, and made the drinks. In one wild week we had a British diplomat who said that the infallible test of a man's class in England was whether he pronounced the word "erotic" with a long or short "o"; a newspaperman who killed himself the next year and left a farewell note, "Don't put Rest in Peace on *my* tombstone"; a Polish playwright who was dissipating his considerable talent by hanging around the rich; the hawk-faced editor of a conservative London weekly who had at his command one of the world's largest collections of scatological limericks; a French banker who could peel an orange so that the skin came off in a single long twirl (he had learned this from his father); my bright young secretary Jennifer, such a pretty girl; a boy from the Abraham Lincoln Brigade who had been badly wounded in the Spanish Civil War; a Yugoslav actress whom we had met in Korcula, and who thought that Ibsen was strictly contemporary; a K.C. from Lincoln's Inn who, before many years, was destined to become Chancellor of the Exchequer; some Broadway show-business people; that fantastic nut Jimmy Sharp, who had covered the war in Ethiopia; and a Chinese linguist-philosopher who had, *mirabile dictu,* recovered recently from an attack of smallpox in Tientsin. Then, too, Mortimer Jackson drifted in—the most distinguished of the Moscow correspondents of that day, who, among other things, was the only authentic bigamist I have ever met, and who, when outside Russia, lived on whitebait, strawberry ice cream, and pecans.

At half-past ten at one of these parties there were still a few survivors and Elspeth put her head in her hands and called out, "Go home, everybody. Party's over, get *out!*"

❋

Mac called me in the office around noon the next day. He had just returned from the lecture tour. All the acerbity that had marked him at our last meeting was gone when we met for lunch. He was as sweet as honey-pie. "I want to apologize to you, Nelson," he said with his smile at its most open. "You were right about the mood of this country, and I was wrong. It's going to take a long time before we're in. Meantime, I think it's the duty of all of us to work for it."

I had scarcely dared to address a word to Karen, or even look at her.

"I've got some errands to do, then see my publisher," said Mac briskly, looking at his watch. "So long, Nelson." He grinned. "Karen, see you at the hotel a little later."

He was gone quickly. Karen and I lingered over coffee, but she stirred with nervousness.

"I don't suppose we can do anything, can we, with Mac in town?"

"Of course not," Karen said, as I drove her to their hotel. "But there's something I'd like you to know."

"What?"

"I love you," Karen said.

She disappeared swiftly through the revolving door.

10

To hear her say that was like being pierced by an electric charge. She had never said these stupefying, apocalyptic words to me before; it may sound silly, but her statement filled me with the wildest kind of unanticipated joy. With a loved one, every second of life becomes an adventure—now I realized the truth of that cliché. I had known that Karen liked me and was fond of me and might even be a little in love with me—after all I'm not a fool—but being in love is no more than the paint job on a house; for her to say that she *loved* me, meaning it in a serious sense, was the cry of heaven, arising out of the inner core. Such words connoted structure, permanence, durability, and Karen was not the kind of girl to use them loosely.

I tasted her words again, and had a tearing desire to express myself. I was *loved!* I shook all over. I could have danced in the street or clapped passers-by on the back or shouted aloud. I felt like a steam whistle with the pressure off. Having been indulged, I wanted more indulgence. I went down to the old Gramophone Shop and bought twenty records, reeling with delight; I drove to a nearby bookstore and ordered everything in sight. At Sulka I bought a dozen ties, and then at a jewelry shop across the street an ornate gold bracelet which I would manage to give to Karen at Christmas, and a handsome ring for Elspeth.

I could not control myself; I took a taxi back to the MacIntyres' hotel; I *had* to see her, no matter what the risk. She drew all the caution out of me. I did not even telephone their room, but, without warning, went up in the elevator and knocked on the door. Mac, in pajamas and a bathrobe, opened it after a wait; Karen was not to be seen. My God, I thought, frozen with dismay, I've interrupted them making love. Mac said ceremoniously, "To what do I owe this honor?" and then, with his hands trembling, poured me a drink. "Karen said you delivered her here an hour or so ago. What's up?" But his tone was warm, friendly.

"Well, as a matter of fact, nothing," I stumbled. "I've just finished some shopping and I thought I'd drop in on the way to my broadcast."

"But you're not on the air tonight!" Mac exclaimed. I was surprised that he knew what days I was on the air, pleased and flattered too. With dread-

71

ful intensity I still wanted his regard. "We listened to you a good deal when we were on the road," he continued easily. "The worse the news got, the more cheerful you became."

I felt that I ought to answer his first statement. "I know I'm not broadcasting tonight, but it's a job, Mac, and I put in hours at the studio every day."

"Oh, I know you're a conscientious bastard." His voice was affectionate. He grinned, but the grin had an edge to it. "About some things, anyway."

Karen came into the room. She did not seem particularly pleased to see me, and she looked wan and tired. We chatted about this and that, whereupon Mac took a piece of paper from his notebook, wrote on it swiftly, and passed it over to her. She stood up, wriggled, and adjusted her skirt. The note said, "Your slip is showing."

Mac said, his voice easy, "You haven't told me yet, Nels, *why* you've dropped in this afternoon—particularly since we all met at lunch an hour or so ago."

"I like the pleasure of your company," said I.

"There must be some other reason."

"As a matter of fact," Karen offered, "I particularly asked Nelson to come up for a drink if he had time—we may not be seeing him again for months."

"You didn't tell me that you had asked him," Mac said, placidly enough. He turned to me. "You're not in love with Karen, are you, by any chance?"

"No . . ." I hesitated.

"Well, if you are, it won't get you anywhere."

Karen said, "If he is, he doesn't know it. He's a little in love with everybody."

"To hell with all of this." Mac slapped his knee. "I'm only teasing, and let's have another drink."

Karen walked me to the elevator after half an hour.

"You shouldn't have come," she said calmly. "That could have developed into a quite nasty little scene. He isn't suspicious really, it was just a shot in the dark, but now I'll have to work a bit to re-establish his confidence in me. He won't let me out of his sight." The elevator was approaching. "Did you hear me *lie?* I do it very well."

"You were marvelous," said I.

"You weren't so fast on your feet yourself, Nels, if I may say so."

"Foot, not feet."

"I feel awful," Karen said. "Oh, darling, if only we could be together."

"Kiss me."

"No, it's too dangerous. Kiss my shoulders, quickly."

"You're a nicely mixed-up young woman," I said, taking leave. "So long."

But actually, as I knew well by this time, Karen was not mixed up at all, but merely the victim of simultaneous conflicting desires. She was remarkably clearheaded, a realist above everything, and she knew exactly what she wanted. The trouble was that her wants were incompatible in their present compass—domestic comity and a free life, security and adventure, Mac and me.

11

Christmas broke its way through the frozen slush, and we slid into 1940. I did not see Mac or Karen for several months. I had to fly out to California for a meeting with our network people there, and I spent some enlivening hours in La Quinta with a marvelous blond movie actress, who had eyes the color of cornflowers and who had the physical trick of being able, so to speak, to turn them off or on. Then came a fast, closely articulated tour by air through Latin America. I crossed the Andes four times—in a DC-3! Nobody had ever heard of pressurizing a cabin in those days, and, climbing the passes, we sucked oxygen out of yellow tubes. The idea was that I should broadcast from a variety of cities, but the technical difficulties were so unexpectedly cumbersome that my talks seldom got through. Karen had managed to telephone me before I left, and I gave her my itinerary. Instantly on arriving in each capital I would tear over to the American Embassy or Consulate hoping for a letter. My avidity to hear from her made me like a man possessed. No word came until I reached Buenos Aires halfway through the trip, and there three letters had arrived and were awaiting me. Almost choking with excitement, I tore them open greedily. It seemed that nothing in my life had any importance except to hear from her. I went berserk with joy.

Children splendid . . . Mac very much on his good behavior, scarcely drinking at all . . . The circumstances of their life were amiable, but rather dull. . . . Gossip about one of Mac's younger brothers, who was working his way through medical school . . . She had enjoyed my letters, but thought that I was going a bit overboard in my praises of her desirability and worth. . . . She had just made four beds (nurse's day off), done the shopping, and put a chicken in the oven. Her signature was preceded by "Much, much strong, sensible, hearty, and tender love, my darling." Then came a pert P.S.: "Lay all blondes."

A letter from Elspeth arrived in Rio, where, in desperate yearning for Karen, I thought seriously of quitting my job, calling off the trip, and coming home. Elspeth wrote:

I may go to the Caribbean for a week, or perhaps Bermuda. I hate it that I'm four years older than you, & I dropped my passport in the bath last night, then changed my birth date when it dried out. A bit messy, but it will do. Now we're the same age.

Just like her, I muttered.

I went to sleep last night thinking of how many proper names I could think of beginning with "Z." I reached fourteen—Zagreb, Zeppelin, Zuleika, Zurich, Zarathustra, Zoroaster. . . . You try it.

Despite myself, I did so. Zeebrugge, Zimbabwe, Zion, Zanuck, Zulu, Ziegfeld, Zola, Zinoviev, Zeus. The letter went on, and my eyebrows perked up.

Mac & Karen have been in town & I asked them to tea. You know how Mac dotes on little ends & odds of what he calls sexual encyclopedism, though it isn't really that. He tipped up my chin and looked carefully along the right side of the jaw, exploring. "If a girl has just made love, there's apt to be a rough patch right there, from the man's beard no matter how closely he's shaved," he pronounced soberly, adding with a laugh, "You're innocent." "Why wouldn't I be?" I replied, a little taken aback. "All women are weak—weak," was his answer. I suppose he's never got over that first wife of his, what was her name, Kathleen, that tall serene girl who went to bed with the iceman and the taxidriver. "Is Karen weak? Does Karen ever have a patch on her skin?" I asked. He became quite angry at this, & I thought Karen looked a little strained. Of course they're *at* each other all the time—it's a form of love play, I suppose. They make love too much.

I made an unpleasant sound.

I think that what I admire most about Karen is her boldness, her directness, an unfeminine quality, but this doesn't keep her from being extremely feminine. Her eyes filled with tears at one remark I made—I forget what. Perhaps, speaking of boldness, one always admires people for qualities one does not possess oneself. To a person like me, so full of doubt & hesitation, always trembling at nuances, it's a matter of wonderment that anybody can be so assured, so positive, even though she's Mac's total slave.

I turned a page.

Mac certainly is still just about the most touchy & envious man I ever met. I took him into the bedroom and opened the safe to show him those Indian jewels you brought me, & he tossed the whole lot down on the bed with contempt & anger, saying they must be fakes!

Then later he apologized & said, "It's strange, isn't it, that Nelson & I always *like the same things*."

I asked him if he had any thought of returning to fiction & what themes attracted him & he astonished me by saying, "There's only one serious theme for fiction, adultery under Christianity." I was rather bright about this & said that I thought we really had progressed a bit beyond Anna Karenina & that the concept of punishment, implicit in his remark, was thoroughly outmoded now not because of religious or ethical considerations but because science proved nowadays that cause & effect are capricious, not determined. Am I right?

Elspeth always had an unerring capacity to spoil. The letter went on:

We talked at great length about you, of course. And I wonder, darling, if you don't see too much of Karen. She's quite capable of using your devotion to her as a kind of spur to Mac, to make him jealous, & God knows he's enough of a jealous type already. Incidentally, he didn't criticize you directly, he's too fond of you for that, but he did say that he thought that you were somewhat obtuse.

What did Elspeth mean—"see too much of her"? Had she caught on to anything?

No, that was impossible.

And what was this about being obtuse?

When they left Mac said something quite odd, & I don't think I like it. In fact it has perturbed me ever since. He said, "Take good care of Nelson, but don't be too much of a hair shirt." Now, really, darling, I'm not *that,* am I? Have a good time, find out what the reasons are *behind* this new Good Neighbor policy of ours, be wary of the senoritas, and come home soonest. I want a ride on Pegasus.

I crunched the letter in my fist harshly. Pegasus was her private name for my penis.

*

Obtuse? Karen and I had made the most elaborate secret arrangements to meet the instant I returned from South America. Mac was doing another lecture tour, and would be in Palm Beach, Florida, on a certain day in February. The lecture was an afternoon engagement, not evening, and Karen was to beg off going on the ground that she had a headache or upset stomach. I kept that date fixed and firm in my mind, and adjusted my whole trip to it, punctiliously, dutifully. On the correct morning, having landed in Miami from Haiti, my last stop in Latin America, I hired a car to drive to Palm Beach, arriving right on the designated minute. My heart thumped as I walked into the small hotel where the MacIntyres were staying. I called their room. No answer. I called again—every fifteen minutes. Still no answer. Yet I knew, I *knew,* that Karen must be there. Time was slipping by, and soon Mac would return, his lecture over. Of course he knew that I would be there; that was part of the plan. I had wired him from Haiti, as I approached home, saying that Karen had written me that they would be in Palm Beach at about the time I was scheduled to arrive there, and could we meet for dinner. His cable in reply said, "Whoops!" But she told me later, much later, that when my telegram from Haiti came, he looked solemn for a moment, distant and solemn, and muttered, "Strange . . . strange."

But it would ruin everything if she did not let me see her before he came back from the lecture, if only for a moment. I was mad to have a word with her. But she was not answering the phone. I didn't quite dare walk up to their room. Already the desk clerk was looking at me with some suspicion.

At last she answered. I talked in as low a voice as possible on the open house phone.

"I was asleep," she said calmly. "I didn't hear the phone."

Of course she had heard the phone. I could have wrung her neck. I had traveled 24,000 miles since seeing her and had kept an engagement made months before with immaculate precision, and yet she hadn't heard the phone.

"I'll be down in a moment," Karen said. "Just give me a moment, and I'll be down."

She must be frightened. Our duplicity was giving her a renewed sense of guilt, and, I thought, this meant that I must be very, very careful. "Goddamn it, she's a bastard!" I said to myself, raging.

But she wasn't frightened at all; she was calm, cozy, and, as far as any external evidence was expressed, very glad to see me. "Mac'll be back in a minute," she said in her low, rich voice. "Nothing's possible here, but I'll be in New York next week, and I'll call you." She hesitated a second. "If I can."

Mac arrived, and we clasped one another and sat down to drinks. He had four martinis, passed through a woozy interlude, and then became testy and arrogant. First came the boasting about women, a standard procedure, and then a forecasting of his own immediate future if, as he then put it, tapping a glass, "this stuff doesn't get me." This was the first time I had ever heard him concede that alcohol might be dangerous to him, or in fact constituted a problem at all. We gossiped about our friends, and he mentioned that he had just heard from London that Enid Scott, the wife of one of our best friends there, Gilmore Scott, had left him. "It must be a hell of a thing to lose a wife if you really care for her," Mac stated gloomily. I said something noncommittal, but Karen put in, "Be careful you don't lose me, Butch."

I was violently torn. I wondered for an anguished second if Mac meant more to me than Karen. I felt a gushing wave of sympathy for him, together with a bitter, burning awareness of my own treacherous hypocrisy and duplicity.

12

I flew up to New York the next day, and set to work
on a group of broadcasts summarizing my experience, such as it was, in Latin America. There were
other professional problems of considerable interest.
We were trying to develop a technique for picking
up news from abroad, from our correspondents in
London or Paris as an example, and sandwiching
them in with my local broadcasts and those by others
on our New York staff; of course this is routine now,
and happens a hundred times a day, but it was novel
then, and demanded an extremely close attention to
timing. In those days if a broadcaster was long and
had a show that was worth it, he was often allowed
to leak over the fifteen-minute period and keep on
talking for a few additional seconds or even minutes,
until his script was finished—how impossible such a
practice would be now! I had to do a good deal of ad-

libbing when a circuit didn't come through and it became necessary to fill a blank where Stockholm or Athens should have been. This was fun.

I recalled the excitement when, the summer before, I happened to be in Moscow on the day of the Russo-German pact; I knew that this meant war and that I must attempt to get out of the Soviet Union at once. I wrote my broadcast and stayed up till dawn to put it on the air, but all the lines across Europe were jammed by military traffic flowing through Germany. I managed to fly out of Moscow to Riga and, the next night, sought to get through from there—again no luck. I proceeded on successive days to Tallin, Helsinki, and Stockholm, staying up most of the night in each, still trying to reach New York. In the end I arrived in London on the last plane from Amsterdam before the war actually broke out, and delivered my piece at last from the bowels of the BBC—the same piece I had carried with me all the way from Moscow—five days late. This was the broadcast about which Elspeth had cabled me, "CRY PEACE."

She was a very intelligent girl, I reflected now, but not logical. Once more I thought of her in contrast to Karen. She had twice the brains Karen had, but Karen was twice the woman.

I finished my second Latin-American roundup, in which I told some rather tepid, invertebrate anecdotes about Lima, Rio, and Caracas. I could not get Karen out of my mind. I began to reflect on aspects of her background—about which, as a matter of fact, I knew comparatively little. She was and always had been somewhat reticent about herself. I knew vaguely that, born in a village in the Dakotas, she had gone to school in Minneapolis. Her father was a surveyor, I believe, or an engineer. She was brought up by a covey of aunts, whom she detested, after her mother died suddenly when she was still young. All her background was primitive, severe; she was a creature of the plains and prairie. Once she told me that if she were suddenly cut off, stranded or bereft, she would return to Montana or Wyoming and buy a band of sheep. Yet some incongruous, mysterious factor made this girl want to devote herself passionately to the study of archaeology, and she set out for Berlin, where she thought she could find the best tutelage, before she reached eighteen. Instead she found Mac. My thoughts went to Elspeth in comparison, a person of the thinnest, most austere New England blood—elite, arid, intellectual, the kind of girl for whom a school like Radcliffe was created. You could have populated Plymouth Rock with her family's seedlings. I wondered how much caste, class, background still had to do with determining the shape of American lives and careers in an era so packed with physical and social upheaval and volatility. Mac—bourgeois, professional, prosperous. Yet he was as unconventional as a goat. Myself—a brat off the Milwaukee streets. Much more than the Soviet Union has the United States produced a classless society or, rather, a society built out of a lot of classes.

I tried to sift out things about Karen. Since I did not hear from her for some days, my misery was boundless, but even so I felt a certain paradoxical happiness, a positive thrilling joy in the mere bare fact that I loved her and was loved. I felt that my love for her justified and excused all my failures and dishonesties; I was exculpated by the phrase, "God is love." *I love you, Ich liebe dich, je t'aime*—this was the one triumphant verity, and it became the sounding board of my existence; I sang with Karen's image in my heart, I slept with a bubble in my blood, and sometimes I did not sleep at all, because I was too happy to go to sleep or, conversely, because I had to stuff a towel in my mouth to keep from yelling. Now I understood why honorable men, in the total embrace of passion, became spies or criminals, cheated friends, sold out countries, betrayed the most sacrosanct of trusts. My physical passion for her remained fixed, dogged, and absolute. All that I knew was that I loved her, and would love her my whole life long.

But I resented it that the most important thing in my life had to be a total secret, and it dismayed me that so many aspects of her character were deleterious. She was packed with faults. My love for her was clearheaded, not in the least distorted by romanticism or blur of focus. If she was a total realist, so was I. I loved her for loving Mac. I loved her for her defects as well as virtues, and sometimes I didn't know which from which. I hoarded every memory of her I had.

There was that time when she was staying with us in Vienna and she had not heard for a week or longer from Mac in Bucharest, where he was chasing a story. "Put me on the Orient Express," she commanded quietly. Off she went without warning Mac, three days on that ghastly creaking train, three nights, and I knew full well that she might quite possibly find him in bed with somebody when she arrived. I went so far as to tell her this, and she answered, "Oh, please don't be cruel—you're hurting me. I *trust* Mac above everything!" I felt that I ought to wire him a warning that she was about to descend on him, but did not do so; luckily he was alone, but drunk. Once before their marriage he had left Berlin on a quick trip to the United States, and did not communicate with her at all; calm as a muffin, she said in the Adlon Bar one night, "If I don't hear from him by tomorrow, I'll know that it's because he's gone to bed with his first wife, and, if he has, I'm going to sleep with the first man I find, but he has to be younger than Mac, because that will hurt him more." Again luckily an ardent letter arrived from him the next morning, whereupon she set sail at once for the United States. He had gone third-class; she traveled first.

A few days after I arrived in New York from Florida, Karen called. I asked, "Where are you?" and she answered, "Here." "Mac?" "In Washington for a day or two." "We might have dinner," I suggested. "That would be very nice," she replied. To have dinner out with a girl meant breaking all the ground rules in my domestic life, but I called Elspeth and made up some sort of story. I met Karen in her hotel, and we went into the bar. We talked animatedly about Mac, her children, my broadcasts, and the adventures of the lecture tour.

"That man's a detective!" she whispered, clutching my arm and indicating a stout man with creased, hanging jowls alone at a table across the room.

"I doubt it. Darling, you're a bit nervous. Take it easy, calm down."

"He's been watching us. He's never taken his eyes off our table."

"That doesn't mean that he's a detective. Matter of fact, if he was, he'd be less conspicuous. It's just your fatal beauty, and he's admiring us."

"I am rather jittery—loathsome word. We can't do anything here. Mac might change his plans and pop in here any minute."

"But I *have* to sleep with you," I protested, reaching for her hand.

"Oh, we're going to sleep together, yes, yes. Why else would I have come?"

I left her for a moment, laboriously clambered out of the bar, and found a suite in the hotel across the street. As a precaution we took different elevators. She tumbled into my arms when we reached the room. "Oh, darling, darling, it's been so long, I've missed you so, darling, darling, I love you, darling."

I did not see her again for a longish time. Mac had asked for a leave of absence after the lecture tour, and he wrote a novel swiftly in a shack they rented in La Jolla, California. Karen loved it there, she was happy, and I was jealous. Mac's novel had, I found out, nothing to do with the theme he had mentioned to Elspeth, but concerned itself with a youthful German student of philosophy impounded into the Nazi movement in Berlin—in the early storm trooper days—who falls in love with a Jewish girl, the daughter of a liberal professor who is sent to a concentration camp. I thought that this was banal, but Mac was skillful with words and might just possibly get away with it. On a gritty afternoon in early April Karen's low, level voice floated toward me through the telephone. Once more they were in New York just for a day. She said that it wouldn't be possible for her to see me, since their stay was so brief, but I pleaded and argued and at last she gave in. It was difficult this time to get a hotel room on short notice—the city was full of conventions—but I managed it. We made love, she was thrillingly sensitive, exquisite, and accomplished, and later I watched her delicate body, with the small high round breasts, so firmly separated, in the mirror on the dressing table. "Well, that *was* nice!" she affirmed.

"Karen, you're a bit fat. An inch or two around the middle."

She gave me a startled look, and then sank into a chair and put her forehead on her crossed hands.

"I'm pregnant," Karen said.

I felt as if I had been kicked. After a moment I controlled myself.

"Could it be mine?" I said.

"No. Chronologically impossible."

I didn't know whether to be relieved or not. "Well, for God's sake!" I exclaimed.

"Please don't let this do anything to you, to us," Karen said. "I hate pregnancy, but I want another child."

She called me the next morning. At the very moment when I was wondering how usual it was for a girl pregnant by one man to sleep with another, she said cordially, "Oh, I feel wonderful!"

We had a bite of lunch before Mac arrived and she alluded to her pregnancy only once. "Pay no attention. It's just as if I had changed my address."

13

Strong, pressing thoughts of Mac suffused me during the next few days. What an extraordinarily complex person he was, what a combination of envy and generousness, of laziness, indulgence, creative spark, and enterprise. He was passionately intelligent, but lacked inner sense. Often I wondered why he drank so much; obviously he was blotting something out, but what? Could it be his whole stricken self? But he had no valid right to be stricken—he had a pleasant family, an exciting wife, a good job, plenty of money, and a reputation that went around the world. And all of it, as Karen said with vehement resentment, all of it went down the whisky bottle. Of course he had now developed the illusion that people did not know it when he was drunk. He might have been a great man—and he pissed it all away. Such a blatant waste!

Soon I saw Mac in a formidable new context, because the Nazis broke loose in Scandinavia and then the Low Countries and France that spring—events which altered the circumstances of all our lives. The phony war was phony no longer. My own responsibilities on the air increased, and my broadcast time was doubled. A new sponsor offered the network a preposterous sum for my services, and so I worked now under the aegis of a brand of cigars instead of a breakfast food. I suppose there was an irony to this, since I've never smoked a cigar in my life, but I had never tasted the breakfast food either. Now came a big turgid row with NBS about the pattern of my program.

Dan Jacobsen, the head of the network, called me in. He looked like a strawberry, with a round bright pink face and fair hair that seemed almost greenish. He was both tough and ingratiating—an operator. I was having lunch at the Centennial that day with Hume Savage, the publisher, who was trying to worm a book out of me, and I arrived back at the studio for my appointment with Jacobsen a quarter of an hour late. He measured me.

"I know you're a conceited son of a bitch, Nelson, but even so, you have no business being fifteen—no, sixteen—minutes late. I don't suppose it ever gets through to you guys, but I'm one of the busiest men in the United States, and I don't like to be kept waiting. What you trying to do, impress the boss?" He pushed down on the glass panel on his desk with two broad hands so hard that I thought the glass would shatter. "I'm used to talent, to temperament too, but you won't get away with temperament around me." He looked me hard in the eye. "Now tell me why you think you're so superior that you won't permit a middle commercial."

This was an old quarrel, now hotly revived.

"Because I think they're murder, Dan. They interrupt the flow of a broadcast, encourage listeners to turn the damned set off, and generally make for a chaotic effect. I write a careful show, my stuff is laced together with a good deal of thought to organization and consecutiveness, and I don't like the interruption. For a sponsor to butt in and yell about some lousy soft drink or shoe polish, right in the middle of, let's say, a careful account of the evacuation of Dunkirk, or some other enormous tragic or thrilling event, is not only offensive in itself, it's bad show business."

"I wish they'd fire you, Nelson, anything to get you off that high horse of yours. But you have a big expanding audience and people like to listen to you and trust in what you say, God knows why. Especially the women like you—they say it's your voice. How-*ever,* the big brass upstairs and the sponsor both *insist* on a middle commercial, so what do we, as sensible men, do about it?"

"Tell them to go to hell."

"Now, looking at it in the abstract as well as the particular, what's wrong with dividing a show in half? Your organization of material can be just as effective that way, maybe more so. You're always neat. Your appeal won't be affected in any way. Pick one theme or event for the first half, another for the second—makes for variety. Besides, the middle commercial gives the audience a pause, a break, a chance to catch breath and evaluate."

"No middle commercial," said I stubbornly.

"Christ, you're a stubborn dumb big Swede."

"You bet."

"You're a laconic bastard too, aren't you, except on the air. Let's have lunch tomorrow, and don't be late, because I'm going to ask Mr. Big himself, the president of the company, to sit in with us. Here, in his private dining room, at 12:45. Mr. Big wants to ask you a lot of things about the war. By the way, do you know this fellow Hal MacIntyre? His agent is trying to line up a job for him on our European service— supplementary to his regular newspaper job, of course."

"He's tops, the best. But you know that as well as I do."

"I know how he writes, I don't know how he talks."

"His command of the spoken language is adequate," I said with irony. I did a sudden about-face. "Hire MacIntyre and I'll do your damned bloody middle commercials!"

Mac was ragingly impatient to get back to Europe. He called me from Washington that evening, and arrived in New York the next day. Karen, he explained, when we met in a bar, had remained in Denver on account of her pregnancy, and he was pushing off alone. I felt like a telephone without a dial, a clock without a face. I sagged into a chair, dissembled my emotion by telling Mac about my conversation with Jacobsen, and said, "I want five Scotches." Mac turned gravely to the waiter, "Five Scotches for Mr. Nelson, please. Yes, bring all five together." We both got drunk, and had a handsome night on the town. I don't suppose, if you are young enough, that anything on earth is more satisfying than a pub crawl between friends. What Mac liked above everything else except sleep and liquor was to stay up all night. After breakfast I took him to the seaplane base at LaGuardia.

A few days later NBS sent me out to the Middle West to broadcast from a variety of our local outlets —publicity for the local stations. After the show in Des Moines I was called to the telephone, and a pleasant voice said, "Perhaps you don't remember me, but we did meet once or twice in the old days. I'm Kathleen MacIntyre, now Kathleen Stone."

Mac had always said proudly that no one who had met her could ever forget her, because of her sensational good looks. Karen was an attractive girl, but Kathleen was a beauty—how jealous Karen must have been of her on this score alone! She might have been an Egyptian princess, with high tawny cheekbones and a fall of jet-black hair, now beginning to turn a little gray. Could those old stories about her promiscuity possibly be true? Could all Mac's talk about her inveterate looseness have any basis in fact at all? I asked her to have a drink with me up in my room, and she ordered a Coke. I liked her extremely from the first moment, and felt stirred by her. Her manner was serene, easy, and intellectually intimate. Soon we started to talk about Mac and Karen.

"Why did you leave Mac?" I asked.

"I didn't—he left me. I think professional friction and jealousy had a lot to do with it. Probably you didn't know, but I had a job in Moscow too, before we moved to Berlin—I was correspondent for a string of German papers. Sometimes I picked up stories before Mac did, and he couldn't bear it. To be beaten by his own wife—unthinkable. He has to be first."

"Yes, I know."

"Doesn't this put a strain on your friendship?"

"No, not really. We're not direct competitors at all, and if we cross wires in any way, I yield to him. If we're on the same story, we work together."

"You're quite a confident person, aren't you?" Kathleen smiled. My God, her teeth! "Mac hasn't anything like your confidence. He's always afraid of being beaten."

"Is that really so? My experience is that he's usually boiling with sass."

"He's very deceptive. I've known him since he was a child. In fact, we grew up in the same Colorado town, and we were childhood sweethearts, as you've probably heard. He was the most delightful person, really—so inquisitive, so full of life and zest, and, in a way, so untutored and unskilled, particularly about sexual matters." Her memory jumped years forward. "When we split up, he went out and hired a prostitute to live with him for a couple of weeks to save his pride. A strange way of expressing one's pride, wouldn't you say? But he had to have a girl, even if she was a whore. Before setting this arrangement up he made the girl go to a doctor and be examined to see that she didn't have any venereal disease. Imagine! It never dawned on him how humiliating this must have been for the girl. I still remember her name—Fräulein Schmidt."

"I daresay we all have our little weaknesses."

"Once at dinner he opened up on me with the air of one who has made a great discovery. He pronounced, 'If orgasms are good between two people, nothing can destroy their relationship or separate them. If they're not good, anything can.'"

"The second proposition is O.K.," I said, "but not the first."

"Of course. But the point I'm trying to make is that he had an obsession about performance." Her olive skin was glowing, and on her lips hung a rueful, affectionate smile. "Not only did he have to be first, he had to be best."

"We know all about his virtues. What do you think is his principal defect?"

"He's a charlatan, an actor. Or perhaps he's simply

carried away by circumstances and the feeling that he must do what is appropriate. It's a quite complex and tenuous thing. Sometimes I remember his wanton, horrid neglect of our little boy, the boy who died. From year's end to year's end, Patrick would never get a letter, not a word from Mac. But then when Mac came home on leave and visited Patrick at his school, how he turned on the charm! He had the headmaster and every teacher eating out of his hand, convinced that here was the most perfect, doting father who ever lived!" I had almost forgotten that Mac had had a son. He never mentioned him or his death, either because the hurt was too severe or because he regarded the entire episode as a defeat.

Kathleen changed tone abruptly. "Is he nice to Karen's children? Tell me about Karen. I've never met her."

I hesitated. Never had I talked about Karen to anybody before; this was a taboo subject, and I didn't want to give myself away. I spoke in a somewhat confused, halting way, mentioning that she adored Mac, had her feet on the ground, and—this slipped out—was possessed of a certain amount of guile.

"How does she handle his drinking?"

"Drinks with him, to a degree."

"That was something I could never do. How did they meet?"

This was one of Karen's most closely held secrets,

but Mac had told me about it, chuckling. One morning a young girl, her hair flying, swept into his office on Unter den Linden peddling tickets for a benefit—something for the colony of Americans resident in Berlin. Mac questioned her, and found out that she had arrived there recently to study Egyptology, because she was determined to be an archaeologist, and Berlin had the best Egyptologists in the world. At once Mac bought tickets for the benefit, and, amused, he asked her out to lunch. She told him later that every American correspondent she had solicited that morning had asked her out to lunch, but she had refused all of them except Mac; she accepted him only because he looked younger than the others. She had never been in a fashionable restaurant before, and he ordered vodka and caviar. She had never had vodka; she downed it with perfect aplomb, as if it were water, and then calmly asked for more. Nor had she ever seen a soufflé before. Mac made lunch stretch until four o'clock, and then suggested that they take a drive along the lakes and have dinner somewhere in the country. She agreed, and then let him take her back to his apartment. The reason she bitterly resented it now when Mac told this story, as he liked to do when he had too much to drink or was showing her off to people for the first time, was that it embarrassed her that she had been such a pushover, so round-heeled, and had gone to bed with him the first time they met.

I gave Kathleen a discreet, shortened version of this story.

After an hour she rose to go. I had the thought, without vanity, that if I tried to make love to her, I might just possibly succeed, but that it would be signally unbecoming for me to have been the lover of both Mac's wives.

I asked Kathleen about her life with her present husband, the man named Stone. He was a contractor, she said—wealthy, stable, decent—and they had two children whom she adored. Wealthy, stable, decent —the kiss of death, I thought.

I took her downstairs and we said good-bye at the hotel door. She asked me to lunch the next day, but I had to go on to Kansas City early in the morning.

"You're still in love with Mac," I said.

"No. I'm fond of him, and I'll always be curious about him and interested in him, but love or in love, no. A person *can* kill love. I took too much abuse."

*

Returning to New York, I found two enormous cartons in the office. It had surprised me that Mac had not thanked me for lining him up for a job with Dan Jacobsen. Here now two gifts were waiting, with graceful, adroit cards. One was the complete Oxford English Dictionary, in all its immensity—the whole set of thirteen stupendous dark-red volumes. The other was a comprehensive set of Landowska albums for Elspeth. He knew from way back that Elspeth loved the harpsichord.

14

Mac certainly had his war now. He missed the fall of Paris, but he caught up with the retreating French on the road to Bordeaux. But this wasn't fighting; it was panic, dissolution. I had a moment of worry about the language problem; he knew perfect German, but not a word of French, not even "*à bientôt*" or "*s'il vous plaît.*" This didn't seem to matter, and his dispatches, like a line unreeling from an inexhaustible ball of cord, were consistently graphic, lucid, and, in the classic manner of American journalism, objective. How we all hated that word because, of course, nothing written by a sentient human being can be truly objective. One can try to tell the truth, but that's something quite different. Arriving in Bordeaux, Mac did his first broadcast for me, and he let himself go—it was a beauty. What he said was, in effect: "Take note of this tragedy, listeners. Note well what happens to a country when its body politic becomes fungoid and rotten with indulgence, rank materialism, and ignoble fear."

I recalled sharply a party in London long before this, a Bloomsbury party full of intellectuals during the Munich period. The conversation reeked of appeasement, and Mac was gloomy, morose, down in spirit. What the guests were saying outraged him, but he strove to be reasonable, as he always did when he wasn't drinking. A Fleet Street editor defended the projected cession of part of Czechoslovakia to Hitler on the ground that this would keep him quiet. "But," Mac burst out, "that's the feed-the-tiger theory. You think that by feeding Hitler you're lulling him into tranquillity, but what you're really doing is making him stronger."

"But what is the alternative?" the Fleet Street man demanded.

"Fight."

"You would seriously consider the possibility of risking war, or even making it?"

"Certainly."

There were squeaks of "Oh!" and "Ah!"

"But we might lose it."

"No," said Mac, with the most earnest gravity, "God would never permit that."

❖

Elspeth was, I have no need to stress, a profoundly stubborn as well as fey young woman. When I first met her, she was much less emancipated in behavior and language than she became. During her analysis it took the doctor four solid sessions of cajolery, pressure, effort, and persuasion before he could make her say the word "fuck" aloud. He had the imbecile thought that this might "release" her. Tonight she turned on the Capehart we had just bought, partly because of the stimulus provided by the Landowska records. We had had a fight the day before because she had painted the brand-new Capehart, with its splendid dark glossy wood, a pale green to match our walls. She did the paint job herself—fearful daubs. I could have strangled her.

Out of a clear horizon Elspeth said, "I listened to you with special care tonight. I think you ought to quit your job."

I was thunderstruck. "Quit my job? And how would we live, if I might ask?"

"Perfectly well on a quarter of what we spend now."

"But quit broadcasting—why?"

"Because you appear to be actively enjoying the dreadful infamy of this war." With interest I recalled that Mac had said some time before that the worse the news got, the more cheerful I became.

"Oh, come, that's not true."

"Your voice makes it seem that way."

I was not so much annoyed by what she said as by the way she said it, with a wicked little smirk of self-conscious superiority. Once again she was demonstrating one of her worst characteristics—her tendency to spoil and reduce faith. I remembered aspects of my life before my accident, in our old place in Connecticut, and how I loved tennis and played it fairly well. Elspeth was insanely jealous of the time I gave to tennis. I bought a new expensive racket, which disappeared after a day or two. I searched for it in vain, and asked her if she had seen it. This she denied; then she cringed, muttering like a child, "I've been bad, bad." She had broken the racket in half, stamped out the strings, and buried it behind the zinnias. "Now whip me," she squealed in a tiny, whimpering voice. In disgust I walked out of the house and took the next train back to New York.

"Nor do I agree with your general point of view about the war," she asseverated. "I think that Britain, not Germany, caused the war, by denying the Germans their legitimately justified need for *Lebensraum*."

That there was a minuscule grain of truth in this made me even angrier than I would have been anyway. I detested her taut, tense fragility.

"You wouldn't enjoy being gobbled up by Hitler," I said, trying to control myself.

"He's no worse than a sodden old imperialist like Churchill. All this talk of fighting for freedom, and look at Palestine and India, to say nothing of Ireland —all enslaved by the British."

I stamped out of the room.

❋

The studio sent me on the road again, this time to visit some of our West Coast stations, and it was easy enough to route myself through Denver, where Karen was staying with Mac's family. She met my plane, and I saw how her coat was swelling over the mound of her tummy. We were close to Thanksgiving now, and it was cold at that altitude.

Karen said briskly, "I had the most dreadful thought as that plane of yours gave a big wobble and lurch coming in to land. If it crashed, I wondered if I could keep your name off the passenger list."

"How sweet. What a darling girl you are."

In my hotel bedroom we lay close.

"When is this large and important event supposed to occur?" I asked.

"Any moment, the doctor says."

"How jolly. Should we be doing this?"

"Now I want you." She rolled over heavily. "Now I don't."

Then she lay back happy, serene and relaxed but panting a little from the heaviness. On my knees, bending over, I began to kiss slowly the round smooth solid melon of belly. I slid my lips from one side of her belly to the other, kissing her gently, and she began to babble, actually babble, in a soft mono-syllabic monotone, almost as if she were whispering a chant. "I've been so lonely, oh, darling, darling . . ." I saw how her umbilicus, a soft dimple, had become a large taut oval, and her breasts, so crisp, so delicate, now bore broad aureoles around the nipples, once so pert and pink—olives now, not *fraises des bois.* I continued to kiss her, from one slope of the high belly to the other, softly, with none but the gentlest, most tender pressure. And this carried me out of myself and I began to address the child within. I whispered endearments to the child, quiet exhortations, messages of affection and good will, promising my love. I felt that the unborn child was a tangible living presence separated from me only by the film of the mother's flesh, and that I could communicate with it and embrace it with all the emotion which flowed from me endlessly. Between us I felt again nothing but the thin, lustrous body wall. I embraced the child through the skin with my chin, my hair, my eyes. I tried to join it there, swelling within the hill of womb.

An hour later Karen said, "I think it's happening."

"My God!"

She picked up the phone, perfectly cool, to call her mother-in-law. "I dropped into town to have a swim here at the Y, which Dr. Andrews recommended," Karen said. "It's starting. I'm perfectly all right, quite capable of driving home, but I'd like to hurry and I think I'll go straight to the hospital from here. So will you telephone the hospital, please, Dr. Andrews too. Thank you. I'll be at the hospital in twenty minutes."

I heard old Mrs. MacIntyre say, "Perhaps I'd better pick you up at the Y, and we'll go to the hospital together."

Karen grimaced. "No, please. This way it will be quicker."

We dressed with alert speed, and I saw her off in her car. Now she looked tense and on edge.

A telegram reached me in Beverly Hills the next day: "FALSE ALARM I FEEL AN UTTER FOOL."

I could not work, think, or sleep.

Three days later came a second wire:

SEVEN POUND GIRL BORN EIGHT THIS MORNING AND I BORNED HER MYSELF DOCTOR JUST WATCHED AND DIDNT HAVE MUCH ELSE TO DO NO MANIPULATION QUITE TIRED AND PLEASED BLESS YOU LOVE

15

Pearl Harbor came the next year, and the national pace accelerated—so did the tempo of our love affair. Karen's governess, Miss M., quit to take a job as a riveter in the Boeing factory in Seattle, and it was impossible to find a satisfactory successor. Karen moved into a small house of her own in the Denver suburbs, and now she had the full care of the children as well as other household chores. She taught herself to be a quite good cook, and of course she was maddeningly neat, as always. "I learned what marriage meant that year," she told me later. "What's more, marriage with a husband five thousand miles away." On my side my professional duties multiplied, and, when priorities in airplane travel began to be enforced, it became increasingly difficult for me to fly to Denver. Even the lowliest lieutenant could bump one of the best-known of commentators.

("Commentator"—how I detested that pretentious word.) Nevertheless I managed at the cost of much inconvenience and considerable risk to my job to fly out to Denver in total secrecy no fewer than twelve times in the next three years.

Prince, now almost seven, shrieked out, "Look at your funny foot! You have a funny foot!"

Devlin said winningly, "You are a very handsome man. I like men with such fierce red hair."

The baby, Deirdre, did not yet have the capacity for understandable speech.

Between trips I deluged Karen with letters, telegrams, flowers, gifts. On her birthday each year I sent her the same telegram: "WITH MY ABIDING LOVE ON THIS FINE DAY." I had the children's birthdays to remember as well, and there were Easters, Christmases, and Thanksgivings beyond numeration.

Mac was stationed in London now, and his work remained first-class. The novel he had written was published at last, but it did not do well; the onrush of events drowned it. No one gave a damn now about Brown Shirt boy and Jewish girl. There were things more immediate and salient to grasp. I had the feeling that Karen was somewhat relieved by the book's failure. She didn't particularly like Mac to write novels—perhaps because she had the subconscious fear that some inner truth revelatory or even damaging about them both might seep out.

During that first year of the war the accent was concentrated on the Pacific, and I had several trips there. Elspeth said, "I don't think you contrive it that way, but it is quite remarkable that everything that happens seems to broaden your horizon and serve your ends. But you neglect *me*, darling."

Two letters from her were delivered to my office on successive days that winter. One was a weird longhand scrawl in the form of a circle with spokes, like a bicycle wheel. Around the circumference and along the spokes were scrawled over and over the words, "I'm frightened." I did not feel pity, but distaste—almost disgust. She was seeking once more to trade on weakness. I called her up and told her rudely to stop such nonsense. The letter that followed was a curt pair of lines on the typewriter complaining of my lack of interest in her, and asking for a bit more intimacy. It concluded, "Is this too much to ask of a man with, so far as I know, no external calls on his spermatozoa, and the usual number of balls?" I gave a somewhat hollow laugh.

In London, Mac was grouchy. I talked to him occasionally on the intercom. I had heard on the grapevine something I didn't like, and which I could certainly not mention to Karen—that he was having a bang-up love affair with a young woman well known to the more unconventional elements of London society, by name Lady Angela Smith-Procter. Of course he always chased grummit, which was our word for tail at the time, but this affair had reached a "serious" stage, I was told. I was furious with Mac for betraying Karen and at the same time sensitively conscious of how this might influence the situation, if you could call it that, between Karen and me.

In any case I found that I simply could not any longer take my happiness, my essential stake in the joy and value of life, in secret bits and snatches. I was stifled, suffocated. I had to be able to breathe again, no matter what. The next time I flew to Denver it must be, to put it coarsely, make or break. I felt so agitated that, absurdly, like a schoolboy before an examination, I made out a little card of notes, a kind of agenda, when I set out, of things I had to say. She did not meet my plane, and when I rang the doorbell at her house, she was sweeping the kitchen floor in an old black sweater and pants with her hair a mess; seeing her this way, I think I loved her more than I ever had before. During two days I scarcely saw her alone, except for one blessed hour at my hotel, because she could not leave the children and was properly apprehensive about admitting my presence to Mac's parents. Desperately I had to be reassured about the reality of her love for me; I had to hold onto this, or otherwise become insane. When I gave expression to this unhappy thought, her answer was, "I must say you've become a bit touchy, Nelson." I jumped as if bitten. Touchy! My soul was being murdered. Then she added calmly, "If you didn't press me so hard, I'd love you more."

We talked about Mac. The last time he was home he had behaved dreadfully, Karen said—bored and irritated with the children, because, as he put it, they disturbed "us," and furious because, although she had her hands more than full with domestic duties, she had taken on a job, and was working as a nurse's aid—part of the war effort. Then, too, he resented it as an affront that she was having the house fixed up—a paint job, minor repairs, and the like. Of course this was for his own future comfort as well as hers, but he didn't see that at all. I expressed my concern and sympathy. "Well," sighed Karen, "you don't always fill your hand."

"You could fill a new hand. Will you marry me?"

"Now, come, Nelson, you're window-shopping. That's not a real offer, if only on account of Elspeth."

"I could make it real."

"Please, no, please. You're torturing me. I have enough on my conscience as it is. Don't turn me into a breaker-up of families, though, frankly, neither Mac nor I can understand why you didn't leave Elspeth years ago."

"If you won't marry me, Karen, what do we do? We've tried it the French way all these years, and it just doesn't work out."

"Not *all* these years. It's been two years, ten months, seven days."

"That's quite a long time for a love affair, an illicit love affair."

"Please, don't wound me, Nels. You're my hold on reason. Maybe I can't be in love with you both, that takes two people, but I love you and I simply can't face life without you."

"You mean you can't live without us both."

"You want easy solutions. But solutions don't as a rule come easily to difficult problems, which is why it's so hard to become wise. You won't face it that life is terrible."

"It needn't be necessarily."

"Wouldn't it be nice to be able to think that?" She hesitated. "Don't you wish me dead sometimes? There are hateful days occasionally when I wish that both of us were dead. Sometimes I feel that I'm crawling back into the dead of night, into a kind of dead blackness, but the children keep me from that kind of nonsense most of the time. What's the simplest poison?"

"I'm a whole man. I want a whole woman."

"You're not a whole man, on account of Elspeth. Do you know"—the sequence of thought was obvious—"that I've even become fond of Elspeth, because she loves you in her crazy way, really cares for you? Tell me—do you love me most in winter or summer?"

"All the time, every minute, every day."

"I love you most when I'm with happy people, and when I'm in the country."

"Please move out to the country at once," said I, "and surround yourself with happy people."

She said sternly, "We must fall out of love, because if we don't, we'll marry, and we can't marry." She laughed. "Tell that to Louis B. Mayer. Will you always love me, be good to me, as you are now?"

"Yes, if only because I have the rather naïve feeling that I can win you by the power of my love."

"You put me under an awful lot of strain, darling. It's not easy to keep pretending to Mac that he's the center of the world, that I'm just a moon revolving around his sun, and playing the role of the utterly devoted slave of a wife, when I'm madly attached to you. Then, too, I feel a tearing hurt within myself at what I must be *doing* to you, making you suffer. I hate to think that I have such power over you. Could you ever be happy without me, do you think?"

"No."

"I suppose I ought to be happy to hear you say that, but in fact I'm both sad *and* happy."

"What a mess!" I said lamely.

"And I won't, I will not, have a tragedy!"

Of course what she meant by not having a "tragedy" was that she would give me up rather than risk a showdown with Mac. I said good-bye, despondent, and she began to weep helplessly. I felt now that I had lost her. This was nothing new, but I had never altogether accepted it before.

＊

Yet I would not give up. Even though Karen had given me no faintest indication of encouragement, I sensed that my position was even more hopeless than heretofore unless I became a free man at once. In spite of what Karen said, I must divorce Elspeth. The only thing to do was to be brutal—cut the

114

umbilical with Elspeth and cut it fast. I felt slightly mad. I had bought Elspeth a new place in Connecticut, on the Sound, which she loved, a big wooden house on stilts for the high water, with hurricane windows stored in the basement. She was basking on an old seesaw, head down, and looked up startled, then wildly pleased, when I clambered out of the car I had taken from the New Haven station.

I remembered some aspects of our former life. We slept in adjacent twin beds, and night after night for years I waited till I was certain that she was asleep and then with the utmost caution and delicacy I would reach out and touch her hand or shoulder with a probing finger, then withdraw it hastily, in dead silence, to find out if she was still warm—with the wild twisted hope that she might be cold, that she might be dead.

She made me a cup of tea, and a crumbling bit of old sponge cake went with it. What she ate had always been a mystery to me. Mostly she ate nothing, although she had a perfectly good digestion. She was an ulcerish type of girl, but had no ulcers.

"I don't want to beat around the bush," I said as soon as serious talk was possible. "Let me come out with it. Elspeth, dearest, I've fallen in love. There's this girl to whom I'm totally committed, and I wonder if you'll give me a divorce."

"A *divorce?*" A purplish blotch, like an aster, appeared on each cheek. She swallowed. "I don't think there's ever been a divorce in my family."

"Darling, your family has nothing to do with this."

"You mean you want to marry somebody else?"

"Yes."

"But I'm your wife." It was most disconcerting, but she burst into bells of laughter. "You, Nelson, are thinking of *marrying* somebody? Preposterous!"

"This is no laughing matter, please."

Her eyes became slits. "Love is good, everybody should love, but that's a personal thing, whereas marriage is serious, it's institutional. Who's the girl?"

"My dear, I'd like to tell you, but I can't—I'm bound to secrecy."

"Then it must be somebody very close, whom I know, which I think unlikely, or somebody celebrated. Eleanora Duse, if she's alive? Some Rockefeller? Mrs. Roosevelt? Some girl at Polly Adler's? Queen Marie of Rumania? Tallulah? Claudette Colbert?"

"Oh, come, Elspeth."

"No name, no divorce."

She quieted down later and said through thin lips, primly, "I shall be glad to be rid of you at any time."

I said, "You are the only person I know who is not merely a lady but a gentleman."

Returning to town, I felt like a monster, but I had achieved my objective—or so I thought. I talked to Aaron, our lawyer, and he decided that the best interests of everybody lay in making the break complete at once. I made arrangements to vacate the big apartment on Central Park West, and asked Elspeth to come into town. "Aaron will tell you about the money arrangements, you'll find them generous, and as to the things here, you take anything and everything you want, except the pictures I bought in London." This offer she refused to accept, and we spent a mortally long anguished afternoon going through all our possessions of many years, dividing them. She took most of the records, I took most of the books. The furniture, the huge sofas, the rugs like warm snowfields, my Spanish chairs and tables, the kitchenware, the beds and quilts and *plumots*, we appraised, catalogued, and divided, a process like the murderous cracking of the shell on a living body, the splitting of a carapace. I ordered two moving vans, and sent everything that belonged to me into storage, since I intended to live in a hotel for a time. During this whole performance Elspeth was quite calm, interested, and steady. At the very end she started to cry, and then picked up a coat hanger lying on the empty floor. I turned, not knowing what she wanted it for, and she started beating me across the shoulders with it, then clobbered me on the head. The blows were hard, stinging, and they hurt.

The superintendent called me two days later. Mrs. Nelson, he reported, had not left the apartment. There she still was, he said, squatting on the bare floor of her bedroom, using candles that guttered out one after another at night, since the electricity had been turned off. No food, no drink. The superintendent, a grave decent man, simply could not persuade her to budge, and now he did not know what to do. I called Aaron, then Dr. Crocker. "For God's sake get her out," I yelled.

✱

NBS proposed a brief assignment to London, and I telephoned Karen in Denver to say that I was leaving the next day. Apparently she had a grapevine to London of her own. After affectionate farewells to me she said coldly into the phone, "Meet a girl named Angela Smith-Procter and lay her. Very beautiful, I'm told."

16

One afternoon soon after returning from London I dropped in at Olga Tritt on the way to my hotel, and, as a kind of beau geste to Elspeth, bought her a handsome small pin of diamonds and bits of ebony set in the shape of a tiny piano. Her note in reply was: "You should not buy me jewels. You should beat me with chains for being a swine."

Recollection seized me. Years before in London she had had an abortion, which made her sterile. I don't suppose I've ever recovered from my sense of guilt about that, although I had not urged the abortion upon her. Even so, I felt that we were partners in infamy, bound together by connivance in a crime, and perhaps my behavior with her ever since has been a form of penitence for that abortion; it was wretchedly done and the circumstances were grubbily furtive and unpleasant. Nowadays every Park

Avenue physician has a skillful abortionist at his disposal, something very different from the situation in London in the early thirties. Harassed, humiliated, paralyzed with apprehension, I found a doctor at last. He performed the curettage in a barbarous, primitive way so that Elspeth did not evacuate the fetus until two or three days later. I telephoned him in alarm when she developed a fever, and he screamed at me, "Don't talk on the telephone, ye bloody fool." Elspeth refused to concede that she was ill, and one of those evenings we went, with a friend, to see a Noel Coward comedy—one of the worst evenings of my life. I kept reaching for her wrist to try to gauge her temperature. We cried through the laughter on the stage. Never did Elspeth altogether get over this experience, and one residuum of it was that she was never thereafter able to pronounce the word "abortion" aloud; she would stumble at the first syllable, then gag. I will not forget the evening shortly afterward when she ceremoniously handed me an envelope marked "Waterloo Bridge." I looked into it and there was the fetus, bloody and wrinkled, the size of a pecan. I asked her what Waterloo Bridge meant. "Oh," she replied, with her mouth twisted into a horrible little circle, "it's our favorite bridge, isn't it, and I thought it would be nice if you tossed this into the water from there."

A letter came from Karen, wise, mature, benevolent, mostly to confirm what she had said the last time we met in Denver.

I have been miserable and lugubrious since you left, and I cannot tell you what happiness it gave me to see you. What a lift I acquire from your joie de vivre, your vitality. I suppose that's the key to everything, vitality. . . . I tried to summarize what I have come to call boringly our "situation." I love Mac, but I'm in love with you, and I love you as well. Mac loves me, and just possibly he's still in love with me. But I feel that there must not be the slightest possibility of a misunderstanding between us, and so I must repeat what I found it so mournful to have to say, that is, the deep conviction that we can never be married. I do not want to be cruel, but, dear heart, the obstacles are insurmountable. You have to take me as I am. There are even horrid moments when I feel that I cannot keep up this double life any longer, because it is indeed all of that. I have not the strength. . . .

Roughly I brushed this aside. It was far too late to back down now, years too late. She loved me, and I loved her. I would not give her up, or let her leave me.

It may sound incredible, but Elspeth came into town, and, hoping to expedite the divorce by having casual contact with her in amiable circumstances, I asked her to stay a day or two in the spare bedroom in my new hotel apartment. When I returned from the studio the next day, she was nowhere to be seen, although her bag and other paraphernalia were scattered about. I walked to the bedroom door and knocked. No answer. I knew, however, with absolute certainty that she must be there. This was a favorite trick of hers, and it always maddened me. She would lock herself into a room, refuse to answer any call or knock, and sit noiseless for long hour after hour, no matter what was going on outside. I discovered during the course of one of these episodes that what seems so easy to do in the movies, breaking through a door by banging your shoulders at it, is in actual fact an extremely difficult accomplishment. Tonight the door at last opened a crack. "What in God's name is the matter?" I cried angrily. She replied in her sweetest, most dulcet voice, "Since we're about to be separated, I thought I'd go into training for it now."

I had a letter from Mac from Algiers, whither he had flown to cover the impending Mediterranean operation. He seldom wrote, and I tore open the envelope, sealed with a censor's mark, with a good deal of curiosity.

I'm almost reconciled to the Russkies. They want the same thing I do, a second front, and it's outrageous that we don't open one. How can we risk being so mortally slow? There's no real military reason for such delay. If we lose a lot of men on a channel beachhead, that's all to the good—it bloods the others, puts steel into them.

I jack off a couple of times a day to alleviate the boredom and keep myself pure of all the little whores downstairs in the bar and lobby.

I haven't had a letter from Karen for a long time. The other men get mail regularly from their wives and sweethearts, but not me, and it's wounding *per se* and damaging as a matter of status and prestige for me to be so conspicuously ignored. Have you seen Karen? What's she doing?

Now how in the world was I going to answer that?

I glanced at a scrawled P.S. "My best to Elspeth, goose her for me." The handwriting looked very shaky.

17

I sat with Karen in a Denver restaurant decorated with the skulls and horns of wild beasts, after we had been together cozily for most of the day. She had a nursemaid of sorts for the children now, and was a bit freer than before. In fact, she startled and amused me when we met at my hotel in the afternoon, saying that the coast was clear and that all she had to do was to be home before six in the morning, since the girl, a student from a nearby college, got up at seven. Six in the morning!

We talked, rekindling the past, exploring the unexplorable, that is, the future.

"You didn't see that woman Lady Angela in London? I'm still curious to get some direct word about her."

"No, I didn't want to search her out or look her up, and I didn't run into her. I didn't see Mac either, as I told you over the phone. He had left for Algiers."

"Perhaps he took her with him."

"I don't see how that would be possible—she would have to have a very big credential."

"She works for the BBC."

"Is that so? How did you happen to hear about this girl, incidentally? How did you know that she was beautiful and all that?"

"Mac told me about her."

I goggled.

"He got drunker than usual one night when he was home on leave a few months ago—I think you were in the Pacific—and started to talk. He said it all began as a screwing match and then he fell in love with her. We were in a train going up to see one of his brothers in Montana. I passed out in the compartment—vomited right there on the floor."

The next day she arrived at my hotel before noon, when I was still in pajamas. The bed hadn't been made, and I put a "Don't Disturb" sign on the door. I noticed that her fingernails were an opalescent silver, not the usual fire-engine red. She muttered, "We're so damned *married*," as she put on my bedroom slippers.

"Except that married people fight, and there's never been a harsh word between us," said I a little pompously.

"It's a good record, but perhaps you're a bit too tolerant. I'm desperately worried about Mac. News is bursting all over the place, and there hasn't been a story from him in a week."

I knew. Moreover, I knew that he had started

drinking heavily again, and, doing a broadcast for me, I had to cut him off the air because he was clearly drunk and the words were fuzzy. I tried now to steer our talk away from Mac, and the easiest way was to come back to me.

"Darling, what else is wrong with me, aside from being too tolerant?"

"Not much, truly."

"What do you like about me most, if you don't mind such obvious fishing?" Desperately I wanted to be praised.

"The color of your hair and the fact that you've never had a sleepless night. Incidentally, I've been taking Amytal hand over fist."

"You shouldn't. I have a queer apprehension that when this whole business blows up, if it ever does, I'm going to be the injured party."

"We're all the injured party." Sharply she blew cigarette smoke through her nostrils. But then she was sweet, loving, and infinitely tender. "You've never been so lovely," I whispered. Not once did I mention the subject of marriage, and I think this was what relaxed her and made her so pleased with me.

"I wake up with you every morning," she said mournfully when she left me that night, "and during the day I remember all the good things, I count them, and I mark them down for my memory."

She drove me to the airport, after a scare when it seemed that my priority had been canceled; this turned out to be a false alarm, but, my God, what a mess it would have made if I had not been able to get back to New York, since I had a broadcast the next day. My capacity for taking chances was expanding by the yard.

"I know you think I'm appallingly regular, but I do have tenor notes," I said.

"They squeak. Oh, darling, I didn't mean to hurt you."

"You didn't, really."

"I've become a demon. I can't stand myself. Perhaps it's because I'm alone so much."

She told me something that interested me a good deal. She and Mac had gone to a family picnic—she thought that picnics were the most fiendish horror ever invented by the mind of man, as did I. Mac was irritable, restless, yawning. Without meaning to make it a serious gesture, she slapped him smartly on the back, saying, "Well, Ralph!" He took this to be a conveyance of contempt, walked coldly to the car, drove back to town without a word, and refused to speak to her for a whole day.

We stopped for a moment at her house so that I might see the children. Devlin gave me a school tablet, a writing pad, in which she had written: "A small present, becos I only had 5 cents."

In the car again I said, "I've been reading some of your letters, rereading them. They're so characteristic of you, amusing too."

She almost hit a fireplug.

"My what?"

"Letters to me. I must have fifty, maybe more."

She stopped the car. Her face was more shocked than I had ever seen it. "But, Nelson, you've told me repeatedly that you burned all my letters—that you destroyed each one as it arrived."

She was positively agape with consternation.

"I was lying to you. I couldn't destroy them. They were part of me, like my hands or eyes. They're all I have of you. I could no more have torn them up than I could have cut off my other foot."

"But it makes me so frightfully nervous. It's dangerous, very dangerous, to let love letters lie around. You've frightened me."

When I made ready to board the plane, she was still angry and her manner had become cold. "I understand perhaps why you can't get rid of them. You might copy them, if you want. But, dear heart, I really must ask you to destroy the originals, tear them up bit by bit or, better, burn them, at once. There must be some kind of incinerator in your office. Think of Mac."

Always Mac.

"There's not the remotest chance that Mac would ever see them. Think of the logic."

"There is no logic," Karen said.

Back in New York, I felt let down and deteriorated, throttled by routine, stale, devoid of spark or animation. I thought back to episodes in my late teens and twenties, when, heaven knows, I had been lively and enterprising beyond the normal. I recalled how I had conned a reluctant city editor into giving me my first job in Chicago, how I had once performed the feat of getting into the Narkomindel in Moscow without a pass, how I had managed to interview people who practically never saw reporters, from Trotsky to Zaghlul Pasha, how I had walked the shattered streets of Hankow arm in arm with Madame Chaing Kai-shek during a Japanese air raid in the early days of the China "incident." What had caused my disintegration? What had numbed and twisted me, aborted my hopes and brightness, slowed me up? Was it Karen? Was it Elspeth? Was it my lost foot?

Again my thoughts burrowed backward, and I remembered with grim clarity that ghastly December night near Innsbruck in the Tyrol. Mac, Karen, and I were finishing up a brief skiing holiday—they were pretty good on skis, I was terrible—and we hopped into Mac's car to drive on to the Vorarlberg for Christmas. Mac was high, but not drunk. Visibility on the loop-the-loop mountain road was not good, and we skirted precipices. The rule of the road changed, as it does in that part of Austria, and after having driven on the right throughout most of our trip, we now had to transfer to the left, as in England, which was confusing. As we rounded a climbing turn, two parallel tubes of light bore down on us with menacing speed, like twin illuminated horns on some monstrous unicorn. Never as long as I live will I forget those appalling parallel tubes of infernal light, rigid, solid, cylindrical, bursting direfully through the mist, carrying their burden of horror. I was sitting on the front seat next to Mac; Karen was curled up behind, trying to take a nap. Mac jerked our car violently toward the mountain side of the road, but he was too late; we avoided a head-on crash, which no doubt would have killed us all, but each car sliced off the near side of the other, like knives. The sound was that of metal pans crashing down a concrete pit, mixed with shrieks, hoarse calls, and cries of fright. Nobody in the other car was hurt seriously, but Mac had three broken ribs and Karen a gash on the elbow. As for me, my leg got caught under part of the engine, which was pushed right back into the front seat.

*

Jennifer, the bright young girl with long legs who had been a Rockette, and who was helping me with my broadcasts now and acting more as an editorial assistant than as a mere secretary, brought in some strands of ticker tape. When Mac met her, he sensed at once that she had been, or was, sleeping with me, and he said sharply, "You've become a collector. You're disgusting." I could not help but grin at this example of the pot calling the kettle black.

Jennifer saw that the page in my typewriter was still blank, and she said in mock alarm, "Look at the clock, Nelson—we're late."

I nodded.

"I suppose you're having daydreams about that woman. Oh, boy," she added cheerfully, "how I could blackmail you! Sometimes I listen in on your calls to Denver."

Elspeth telephoned later. Her voice was tense, and this was a danger signal. I had a moment of bitter irritation at the nature of women, all women. She asked me if I wanted to see her new apartment, which she had taken at last—an invitation she had never extended before. We drove up to Ninety-fourth Street on the East Side. The house was built in the familiar pattern of brownstones in that area, and I had to climb six or eight steps, which was irksome. Elspeth fished for a key, flung the door open, and clicked on the electric light. I stood back appalled. I was dumfounded. There, piled up, unevenly stacked in cartons, were all her possessions from our former place—books, records, rugs in long sagging rolls, kitchenware, lamps, wastebaskets, various installations, and the furniture. She saw my face, and turned crimson.

"It's too awful of me, but I just couldn't face unpacking and settling down," she explained.

"But," I asked, in a mixture of exasperation, solicitude, and plain dumb miserable shock, "where are you *living?*"

"I stay in the country most of the time. When I'm in town, I go to a hotel."

I protested vehemently, "But you're using an entire big *apartment* as a place for storage!"

She replied, menacingly, "Even though you spend all your money on other women, we can afford it, can't we?"

I slapped her—the only time in my life I have ever slapped a woman. The slap made a resounding crack. She started to cry, and then howled, "Oh, you should have done that long ago!" Same old pattern, I thought wearily.

It fell on me, naturally enough, to fix things up. I got rid of the apartment, and a week later she telephoned me with agitated pride to say that she had found and rented *two* places—one to live in, one as a kind of studio where she could do her writing. I noted the addresses. Her apartment was on Park Avenue a few doors from the new one I had just taken, and the so-called studio was across the street from my office. If nothing else, she was going to get proximity!

Exhausted, I took time out to go to the Waldorf and have a massage. I had been putting on weight, which was bad for my foot. The only trouble was that, immediately after sweating off a pound or two in the electric hot box at the Waldorf, I would invariably saunter into the bar and have a good hearty ham sandwich with a glass of beer, which at once put the weight back on again. Karen was mused by this; Elspeth disapproved.

But Karen was impure; Elspeth, pure.

I remembered Elspeth stretching her slim arms upward, her hair a golden bubble, whispering to me with rapture, "You're the only person who understands the terribleness of me, my weaknesses and all my disastrous faults, and yet you love me, care for me, protect me. Therefore, I am blessed!" I had another memory, too, of the early Connecticut days when, the night before I was to set out on a trip to Europe, we made love, it seemed interminably, and yet I could not physically finish the act. I remained fixed within her; it was as if I were sealing her, stamping her, by the very fact of my incompletion; now she could never be rid of me; she was sealed shut. For, by the physical circumstance of leaving myself within her, I prohibited the entrance of anybody else, making sure that nobody could ever supplant me, replace me. It left me within her always. Well, I was paying for it now.

With revolting weakness, hypocrisy, falsity, I paid court to her for years, and still, as a matter of fact, continued to do so. It pleased my ego to be kind, but of course it wasn't kindness at all. I didn't want to hurt myself by hurting her. I liked to play little games. Only the year before I had walked into a Western Union office at Christmas and sent her the entire assortment of holiday messages available, thirty-seven in all.

Now I did not have the same kind of impulse. It took almost a year to persuade her to go through with the divorce. She fought with Aaron endlessly before finally signing an agreement; when she signed it at last, I had pangs of remorse which almost over-came my exultant delight in being free.

Yet, to gain her assent to the agreement, I had to threaten to go to Nevada myself, throwing my job and career out of the window. And I would have done this, no matter what the cost, if Aaron had not brought her around. She insisted that I see her off on the train. There she stood as it pulled out of Grand Central, a foot on the step, tiny, tousled, and wan; the train gave a puff, she rushed back to the window of her compartment, and made Churchill's V-sign through the glass. Then from Las Vegas a letter came almost every day.

Over the long-distance phone I gave Karen play-by-play details of all this unhappy procedure, and told her what a whopping alimony I had agreed to pay, although Elspeth herself did not ask for any-thing at all. "I wanted to be generous," I told Karen with somewhat vulgar emphasis. "After all, she's the one getting it in the neck."

"We're all getting it in the neck," Karen said.

*

D Day came and went, and the assault on Festung Europa, for which all of us had waited impatiently for so long, began at last. No dispatch came from Mac for a solid week. Karen called me, frantic. "Maybe his copy got lost in the rush," I sought to soothe her. "There must be a huge file of stuff backed up and waiting to get off."

134

But I knew better.

Karen said glumly, as she had said in different circumstances long before, "Thank God for the children." Then she repeated another remark, "Will you *always* be good to me, care for me, love me as you do now?"

I was struck, too, by her reaction to the news that Elspeth had finally agreed to a divorce. She seemed to be at her wits' end, terrified.

18

Mac was fired by his newspaper some time after the Rundstedt breakthrough in the Ardennes. He had stopped working for me some months before, saying that two jobs were too much to handle. His work had been quite good up to the time when Paris was liberated by the Americans, the French, and Mr. Ernest Hemingway, and then disintegrated. He botched several stories during the wild scurry across France in pursuit of the retreating Germans, and then, when his paper rebuked him for having missed some details of the battles in the Hürtgen Forest, he walked out on the story in pique and for a considerable period did not file anything at all. His behavior was that of a spoiled star. Nor did his dispatches have their old punch and clarity; those dazzling classic leads seemed to be a thing of the past. Clearly, he was too full of booze. The only thing for him to do was come home, have a rest, stop drinking, and start rehabilitating himself. Karen waited in Denver—so upset that she came down with a case of shingles—and I waited in New York.

I had a disturbing memory of something he had said to me long before. "If Karen ever falls in love with anybody, I know her well enough to know that she'll go the limit, and then I'll have to kill her." The last letter she had from him accused her of "destroying" him, and that did not make me feel easier.

Perhaps the best thing would be for me to fly out to Denver once more, if only for a day. It was becoming more difficult to telephone long distance; calls were held up for hours. Once Denver reported a sixteen-hour delay. But it was also extremely difficult to get space on an airplane, and I didn't want to risk not being able to return. Then came a telegram from her announcing Mac's imminent arrival, and saying that consequently I must not come. Her wording was peremptory. The only thing for me to do was write a letter. I felt imperatively that, at this supreme moment, I had the right to state my case. Otherwise, I forced a smile, it was taxation without representation. My letter, ground out in passion as it was, was unnecessarily detailed, supererogatory, and prolix. It was certainly the worst letter I ever wrote, as well as the most important. I outlined to Karen the whole course of our lives together, reiterated my devotion, emphasized a hundred facts, places, dates, in our past, and appealed to her to consider very, very seriously the appalling risks and unpleasantnesses she might face if she went on living with Mac. I underlined the fact that I was now a free man, and concluded with what I thought was a light note: "There are 58,980,621 women in the United States, but you are the only one I care for—will you marry me?" Then a postscript: "Don't lose the key to 16G"—the number of my apartment. What the letter stressed more than anything else was the long duration as well as intensity of our relationship. It was one hell of an inclusive letter, I must say.

About ten minutes after I put it in the mail a telegram came from Karen:

MAC ARRIVED HE IS NOT IN GOOD SHAPE AND IS INSANELY SUSPICIOUS AND JEALOUS OF ALL AND SUNDRY EVEN INCLUDING MEMBERS OF FAMILY PLEASE DO NOT REPEAT DO NOT ATTEMPT COMMUNICATE WITH ME IN ANY WAY TRUST ME I WILL WORK OUT EVERYTHING FOR THE BEST

How could I warn her about the long, crazily compromising letter now en route? I settled on the following:

MERCHANDISE HAS ALREADY BEEN SENT AIRMAIL SORRY DID NOT GET YOUR INSTRUCTIONS UNTIL TOO LATE SIGNED BONWIT TELLER

Mac drank himself into a stupor; he terrified the children; he collapsed. Details like these I had from

Karen later. She picked up my letter casually when the mail came, waited till he left the room to go into the kitchen for a moment, read it, and, before she could destroy it by tossing it into the fireplace, heard him return. She skipped to the nearest closet, muttered something about looking for a scarf, and stuffed the letter in a pocket of the first article of clothing she could reach, one of Mac's old tweed jackets. I will give any student in a beginners' psychiatry class a prize of one dollar for working out the correct subconscious motivation for this.

Of course it was inevitable that, within minutes, Mac, about to go out into the garden, should reach into that closet himself and put on that same old tweed jacket.

"What's this?" he said grumpily, returning. "From Nelson? I wouldn't trust Nelson further than I could throw a Tiger tank."

Karen's heart stopped.

With his hand trembling, Mac took the letter out of the envelope, muttering, "Seems to be a longish document. Mind if I have a glance at it? Good man, Nelson, the Old Reliable."

If she had reached over swiftly and snatched the letter out of Mac's hands at that instant, she could probably have tossed it into the fire before he read it. But she was too late.

Mac became pale; he dropped his hands; his eyes enlarged. Rising, he grasped her by the shoulders. "What does this mean?" Slowly the implications of the letter's contents dawned on him. He waved the letter at her, and snarled through quivering lips, "You bitch! You filthy whore and cocksucker! Get out of this house! Strumpet!"

*

I called Elspeth as soon as I heard about this and, very much shaken, asked her to drop in at the office for a cup of coffee. I shooed Jennifer, who was agog, out of the room.

"I don't suppose you've forgotten that I told you some time ago that I was having rather a demanding love affair," I said to Elspeth.

Little beads of sweat formed on her upper lip.

"It's all over now, so I can tell you more about it, if you want to know."

"I'm not sure I do want to know, now."

"The girl was Karen MacIntyre."

I thought she would faint. She rocked on her feet. "What a peculiar exchange," she said at last. "He took your foot, you took his wife." Then: "What can be wrong with me, that I never guessed?"

19

I have mentioned that Mac had a largish family, most members of which lived in Denver or its environs. He trundled Karen into their car, and visited his brothers and a sister one by one. Before each the same scene was performed. The children, if any, were sent upstairs, and Karen was flung, literally flung, onto a chair or couch, while Mac gathered the adult members of the family together and delivered a brief speech.

"Would you kindly look at Karen. I would like you to inspect my wife, inspect her carefully. Perhaps she is not looking at her best. No wonder. My wife, Karen MacIntyre, is a filthy whore and bitch. She has been betraying me for the past five *years*, steadily, deliberately, with my best friend, Nelson A. Nelson. I will deal with Mr. Nelson, my so-called friend, a little later. He scarcely matters. But Karen, the mother of my children, does matter. Presumably, at least, I am the father of these children. How many of them are legitimate I do not know at this moment. In time I will beat the truth out of her. Of course Karen never had an *orgasm* with Mr. Nelson in spite of their profligacy. No, no. She has never had an actual orgasm with anybody in her life except me. Now, I will proceed to give you some of the more revolting details of Karen MacIntyre's criminal behavior during the past five years."

And so on for an hour.

The fifth time this scene took place, Karen, who had seemed drugged, almost comatose, reached for a Coca-Cola bottle, smashed off the top, lunged toward Mac, and stabbed him in the lip; then drew the broken edges of glass across her wrists.

Mac's sister bounded forward, and in a second was tightening a handkerchief and a necktie around Karen's wrists, meanwhile shouting at Mac, "You beast! You horror!"

"A doctor, quick," the brother-in-law exclaimed, grabbing a telephone.

"I won't have a doctor," Mac said loftily, spitting out blood and teeth.

"If you don't, you'll have a harelip all your life, not so good for a man who goes on lecture tours."

A few days later I had a letter from Mac:

Nelson—

I consider you to be a person without honor, a moral

imbecile. I will follow you to the end of your days and shoot you down like a dog.

Moral imbecile. Well, that was nice.

You will learn in good time that I am permitting Karen to enter suit for divorce. I shall not contest for custody of the children.

If you have a spark of decency, which I doubt that you have, you will marry Karen after the divorce. It is the least that can be expected of you. If you were a person of honor, you would commit suicide.

I consider that all our friends will agree that you should marry Karen as soon as possible.

I wrote back at once:

Dear Mac—

I'll be delighted to marry Karen just as soon as time permits, but not for the reasons you adduce. I don't care in the least what friends think or about the conventional proprieties. I want to marry her because I love her with all my heart.

*

That did it. I did not mean it to do it, but it did it.

Mac simply could not bear it that I *wanted* to marry Karen. All his old bristly competitive instincts, his fierce assertion of ego, became involved and augmented. Apparently he chewed on my letter for anguished days, and finally wrote me again, to the effect that he was taking Karen back "on probation" based on the strictest of understandings that she would never see me again under any circumstances or communicate with me or permit communication from me of any kind.

Then—of course!—I had at once a letter from her, a miserable little scrawl, in a handwriting that seemed hardly to be her resolute own:

Dearest Heart—I couldn't leave him in the state he's in—you couldn't leave a sick dog in that state. I have got to give him another chance. Perhaps someday you will forgive me. I love you always.

K.

He was packed off to the psychiatric ward of a Denver hospital, and spent some weeks there. Presently they passed the summer at a mountain camp in Wyoming, and he stopped drinking. The enormousness of his gesture forgiving her gave her a sense of pride and satisfaction, and she sought earnestly to make amends for her life with me by being doubly attentive to him, devoted, and affectionate. The sense of double forgiveness made them both cautious, like people with bare feet on stony paths, who must not take a single step out of line.

As for me, I felt at first like a general defeated in battle by foul means; I had never had the chance to confront him openly, to assert myself and make my case. But that was her choice, not mine, and there was nothing I could do about it. For a time I felt that my brain was being drawn out by a needle; the grief and sense of irrevocable loss left me unutterably drained, destitute. Then for some little time came a period of shadow, blackness, horror, in which I sought to adjust myself to the reality of what had happened. I had not yet fully comprehended what losing her would mean. My brain raced and boiled with demented plans—I could kill him, I might abduct her, I could contrive to have him arrested on some fabricated charge, and sent to jail for a long period. I knew that their Denver house was empty, but I kept telephoning there, giving the number to the operator over and over again with crazed persistence; if anybody had answered, I would have rung off. I trembled when my own phone rang; I clawed through the morning mail like a man haunted or possessed. My yearning, heartbreak, desolation, blotted out every other aspect of my existence; I became a shaken wreck, until at last I felt a modicum of relief. The thralldom was over; I was a free man again at last. But the relief, blessed as it was, so profound that it exhausted me, did not last long.

One of those nights on the air I made more fluffs in a quarter-hour than in the whole preceding year.

20

It was the middle of May now, just after V-E Day, and I reflected without drawing any conclusions that our affair had lasted more than five years and had taken place between dates almost exactly those of the war in Europe. On an hour's notice I flew with a covey of correspondents and broadcasters to have a look at the corpses and dying relics of men and women in one of the first concentration camps opened up by the advancing Allied armies within Germany, and then again, on the invitation of the Air Force, I joined a flight to hover over the smoking ruins of Berlin. When the war ended, I took a holiday, my first in years, near a Vermont lake, a plate of slate, where the dew seemed to be two inches deep on the greenest of lawns, where loons called in the piercing starlight, ducks flew low, otters dove in ponds, deer crossed the roads with timid pride and innocence, and raccoons tipped over garbage cans on the back porch and made a mess.

My period of relief did not, as I say, last long. Not only was I still a man demented, but one inflamed by loss. I went through every sort of trick and subterfuge to try to get in touch with Karen. At the slightest move from her I was prepared fully to dive into the abyss once more, no matter what the risk or what suffering this might entail. In a word, since I knew her well, I still had hopes. But no communication ever came from her until a package arrived in New York months later containing all the jewels I had given her. "Gee whizz!" exclaimed Jennifer. I gave Jennifer a brooch. On the top of the package lay an envelope, which I opened in curiosity combined with a blend of hope and trepidation. It contained nothing but a scribbled note, "This then is farewell," and the key to 16G.

*

On a Sunday with bluff sunny winds I went up to see Elspeth in Connecticut, and stayed the night. I had always supposed that I had a kind of Indian sign on her, but perhaps it was she who had this spell, this incantation, on me as well. Mac and Karen certainly had Indian signs on each other.

I found Elspeth down on the beach looking for seashells. There was scarcely an egg in the refrigerator when it came time for dinner. In contrast I thought of Karen's exquisite sensitiveness to food, her lively appetite and unerring palate. Elspeth apologized for the emptiness of the larder, and explained that she had made a mistake, thinking it was tomorrow that I was arriving, not today. I do not know whether this was true or not, but Karen had never made a mistake about a date in her life.

Perhaps by now I had recovered from the acute stage of my despair about Karen—biting at bedposts, yelling curses on Mac in the middle of the night and sometimes screaming, yes, actually screaming, when I was home alone—but not by much. Steadily I relived every page of my life with Karen, I sought to remember and write down every word she had ever spoken to me. The accommodation to total and irrevocable loss is, I am sure, the most difficult and painful experience that ever comes to a person. I felt utterly lost, abandoned. The only alleviation is that stately omnibus, time, and even that doesn't always work, or works too slowly.

Words reread from her that moved me most were about her children. "My little blossom totters by the edge of the tub when I bathe, rubs soap on my shoulder, and kisses it."

That evening, after a miserable sandwich made out of something in a can, Elspeth, who was looking exceptionally pretty, rose brightly, saying, "Oh, I've never showed you this!" She opened a drawer and pulled out a sheaf of crinkly legal-size paper held by a blue binding at the top. She proffered it archly with false pride. "Look! Our decree!"

The next morning the telephone rang—Karen. My secretary Jennifer, who loves mischief, and with whom I had an engagement for dinner the next night, had given her Elspeth's unlisted number when she called the office. My heart clenched like a fist. I thought it would burst out of its cage of ribs.

Her voice was low, thrilling.

"We're in New York for a day. I'm calling from a booth—I didn't want any notation of a long-distance call to be on our hotel bill. Mac's going to be in Washington tomorrow, and I wonder if we could meet." Her voice gave no intimation that there had ever been any separation between us, no hint of torture, travail, or the long years of satisfaction, agony, companionship, friendship, love. "Perhaps you'd take me to lunch? Yes, of course, Nelson darling! Glad—so glad! Let me think, I don't want to see you in our hotel for some odd reason" (she actually chuckled slightly) "but let's meet at Hampshire House at one. That's off our usual circuit, and should be safe enough. Ah, darling, yes!"

Elspeth was standing in a corner of the room, and must have heard me say throatily, "I'd cross the continent to see you."

Elspeth asked laconically, "Karen?"

I didn't want to lie. I felt bold, excited, exalted. "Yes, we're having lunch tomorrow."

The next morning getting dressed I discovered to my concerned astonishment that my foot was not at the side of the bed in its usual place. Elspeth was nowhere to be seen. After a witless hour searching, I had to give up, sweating, agonized. This was the final infamy, humiliation, degradation. I felt that I had lost the world. I became crazed, distraught beyond endurance. In truth Elspeth had emasculated me at last. Now I became aware that I was indeed a cripple, something that I had never really conceded before. I dragged myself across the room and plunged down the steps, crawling like an animal.

The telephone, attached to the wall, was difficult to reach. "Karen!" I cried when I heard her voice. "Elspeth's hidden my foot! I can't come!"

*

I never saw Mac or Karen again. Presently Mac quit journalism to devote himself to writing novels, at least two of which did quite well. He wrote a successful autobiography too, some years later, in which my name, naturally enough, does not appear. The MacIntyres live these days on Ischia near Capri, and I hear from friends that they have a good life there. Mac is known as the man-who-won't-let-his-wife-out-of-his-sight. Somebody told me some years ago that Karen had had another baby and that Mac, after a Cyclopean struggle, had finally stopped drinking once and for all. So she did save him after all, and that was her triumph, her vindication, the expression of her final will. I often wonder what would happen if we should all meet accidentally someday at a party or in some vacation spot. Meanwhile I tend to avoid southern Italy in general and the Bay of Naples in particular when I take a holiday, not because I am afraid but because I would not like to disturb their tranquillity—if, indeed, that is what they have achieved. I do not feel any sense of guilt any longer. Nothing is anybody's fault if you tell the truth, and if I resent anything about Karen, it is that she would not let me be truthful. Then, too, I comfort myself in a gallimaufry of emotions with the somewhat oblique thought that, after all, I saved their marriage, or at least restored it.

And of course I shall never forget her nor forget that intricately locked procession of glowing, sun-to-moon-whipped years, when every page of her life, every tissue, was interleaved with mine. I have lost her, but not the five years. My God, how I loved her! And I loved Mac too. I still miss him, actively miss him, perhaps even miss him more than her, particularly when comrades from the early days in Europe gather together, or when I lay siege to the giant body of sleep, but cannot sleep.

I do not suppose that I will ever recover from Karen fully, nor do I want to recover. Perhaps it saddens me to know that, even if I should ever fall in love again, I could never possibly recapture or duplicate the russet glow, the flush, the radiance and ecstasy of our experience together. If I ever saw her again, I know perfectly well that my heart would resume peremptorily that turbulent and greedy beat, that I would throb from skull to toe at her slightest smile or gesture. She made me full, and I still feed on her. Meanwhile there is much else to concern and occupy me, to assist the ineluctable passage of days melting into each other. I suppose it was inevitable after Mac and Karen left the country for good that I should begin to think of remarrying Elspeth. Man is not made to live alone, and a large part of me belonged to her. My respect for her sense of fundamentals had never declined, nor my delight in her wit and brightness, her unexpectedness and capacity to extract pleasure from the harshest texture of the philosopher's stone to the powdery glitter of a moth's wing. And perhaps it was a challenge to think of the possibility of resuming responsibility for anybody so wayward and errant, so given to the appearance of frailty but with such a solid appreciation of things basic and the achievement of her own ends.

Actually, I realized now that she had more realism in her than Karen did, and she was supported by a substructure of conviction and regard for truth that Karen altogether lacked. I had a sudden memory of that day I spoke to Karen for the last time from the house in Connecticut. Elspeth said when I put down the telephone, "You don't look like a young man any longer."

70 71 72 73 74 8 7 6 5 4 3 2 1

In this suave, wry novel of illicit love during the Second World War, Mr. Gunther has created four unusually complex characters—a cripple, an alcoholic, a schizophrenic, and a headstrong young woman, all, however, very nice people—working out their problems against the urgency and fears of the time. It is a double-decker story in which the bizarre interactions among the characters seem to belie their inherently agreeable qualities.

Nelson, a highly successful radio